IRON WILL

LORDS OF CARNAGE: IRONWOOD MC

DAPHNE LOVELING

ISBN: 9781090224156

CONTENTS

To everyone who struggles to keep their heads above water.

The Ironwood is a slow-growing, medium-sized, deciduous hardwood tree. It is the hardest, densest wood in the world — so dense and heavy that it will not even float in water. It's durable and holds up well under pressure and strain.
For all its good qualities, ironwood is tough to work with. Some woodworkers say it is similar to working with stone.

LORDS OF
IRONWOOD
CARNAGE

PROLOGUE

The girl is slight of build. Tangled, hay-colored hair. Dirty pink undershirt.

A pediatrician would tell her mother that she is underweight for seven years old — in only the twentieth percentile for her age group. But her mother can't afford to take her to the pediatrician.

The girl, whose name is Paisley, crouches in the corner, in the small space between the wooden nightstand and the wall. She's hoping Mickey will forget she's there. He's on the phone, angrily shouting, his voice bouncing off the thin walls of the motel room.

The girl's mother isn't here. The girl's mother doesn't know Mickey has come back. Mom kicked him out last night. But this afternoon, when Paisley got home from school, he was here.

"I told Jimmy not to fuckin' worry!" he's yelling. "He... ah, Jesus Christ, Dewey, I ain't got it right now! Tell him to chill the fuck out. Naw, man... Bethany's got the car, I ain't... God *damn*it, Dewey, what did I tell you? *What did I tell you?!*"

Paisley doesn't want to be alone with him when he's like this. When he gets off the phone he'll be raging, and she'll be the only one here. But he won't let her leave without a good reason.

Desperately, she tries to think of a way to get outside and away from Mickey until he calms down. She looks around the room, casting about for an excuse, when suddenly, an idea comes to her.

Maybe it will work. If she doesn't get scared and mess up.

Crawling up off the ground as Mickey continues to shout into the phone, Paisley goes to the dresser. She opens the bottom drawer, where her mom keeps the dirty clothes until it's time to wash them. Paisley finds a couple of plastic shopping bags in there, and stuffs some of her own shirts and jeans inside. There's a small zippered pouch with quarters in it, and she takes that, too.

At the last second, she turns and grabs the worn chapter book she was reading in her hiding space. She's read it a dozen times at least, but it doesn't matter. It's the only book she owns.

Paisley does all this as quickly and quietly as she can. She shoves her feet into her worn sneakers and moves toward the door. She's careful not to look at Mickey, hoping he'll ignore her. He's still on the phone as she slips by. But when she puts down one of the bags to open the door, a rough hand shoots out. He grabs her roughly by the arm and yanks her toward him. She winces but manages not to cry out. It's her bruised arm — the same one he grabbed her by last night.

"Where the fuck are you goin'?" he spits at her.

"To do laundry. Mom told me to do it while she was gone," she lies.

He yanks harder, pulling until her face is inches from his. She can smell his breath, his sweat. She tries not to flinch. She keeps her eyes on the wall, but when he doesn't let her go, she risks a look at him.

"The fuck are you lookin' at?"

"Nothing," she whispers, looking away again.

With a final shake, he lets her go. Barely daring to breathe, she opens the door and scoots through it. She grabs the second plastic bag and pulls it through with her. The bag catches against the latch as the door closes, ripping and spilling the contents on the ground. Hurriedly, she scoops up the clothes and gathers them into her arms.

The girl steps quietly out into the exterior hallway of the motel complex, letting the door slam shut behind her. The room that she, her mother, and Mickey live in is on the second floor. To get to the cold, cement-floored room where the washing machines are, she has to carry the laundry down a flight of rickety stairs.

The quarters make slight ticking noises in her pocket. It reassures her to hear them there.

As she starts down the stairs, she realizes she forgot to look for laundry detergent. She's afraid to go back inside the room, though, now that she's escaped once. She decides she'll try to find some downstairs in the laundry room. Or maybe she can ask to borrow some from somebody. If she can't find any, maybe she can just wash the clothes in water. But no, there are stains on some of them. And she doesn't have anything clean to wear tomorrow. If she has to wear dirty clothes, the kids will notice.

Paisley's face flames hot with shame at the thought. The kids in her school make fun of her enough as it is. They taunt her for her dirty jeans half a size too small, and her scuffed-up discount store shoes. The stinging barbs of her classmates are burned into her mind. Today, Callista, a girl with always-perfect hair and expensive clothes, wrinkled up her nose and told Paisley that she smelled.

Mom and Paisley have never had a lot of money. But now that Mickey's around, it's worse. When Mom got mad at Mickey last night and kicked him out, Paisley prayed in her head that he was gone for good. It was better when it was just her and Mom.

God must not have heard her, though.

There's no one else on the stairs when Paisley starts down them with the clothes in her arms. The mound of laundry is so big that she can't see her feet, so she has to feel for the next step with her toes. One step down. Then another. She leans against the banister for support. Another step.

Then, the banister, poorly attached to the wall, slips under her weight.

Paisley starts to tumble, her arms letting go of the dirty clothes as she splays them out and tries to catch herself. She cries out as she falls sideways, down the stairs. Her body instinctively tries to turn itself, but there isn't time.

She lands on her left side three steps from the bottom, her shoulder making a sickening crunch against one of the wooden steps. Her side falls against the one above it. Her head knocks hard against the ground as she comes to a rest. Searing pain rips a scream from her young throat.

Paisley's body comes to rest at the bottom. Her whole left side is agony. Her head feels fuzzy and pounds so hard she feels like she might throw up. And then, just as the thought makes itself known, she leans over and vomits onto the pavement.

Upstairs a door opens, then shuts. Someone comes running down, making the stairs shake.

"Oh, shit, you okay?" a teenage girl wearing too much mascara gasps. She peers down at Paisley, her eyes wide.

Paisley starts to cry, but the crying hurts her head. She hurts so bad, and Mickey will be mad and call her stupid and useless. For a second, she thinks maybe she can just get up and it will be okay. But when she tries to move her arm and sit up, she cries out in pain again.

"I'm gonna go get my mom," the teenager blurts. Her words reach Paisley through a thick fog, barely registering.

A few seconds later, a rotund woman with beady eyes, who must be the teenager's mom, comes out. As soon as she sees Paisley's arm, bent unnaturally and already turning colors, she gasps.

"Honey, is your mama around?"

Paisley starts to shake her head, but it hurts so bad that she leans over again and dry heaves. The woman bends down and sits on a step with difficulty, then puts a kind hand on Paisley's back. Paisley is full-on crying now, trying to stop herself and wiping her nose on her forearm as she hiccups and sniffles.

"We're gonna get you to the hospital, honey," the beady-eyed woman says.

Everything someone says to her feels like it's in another language. Before Paisley can process the woman's words enough to answer, the manager trots around the corner, followed by the teenager. He takes one look at Paisley and the woman and splays out his hands. "I can't leave the office!" he stammers.

The woman mutters a curse. "Worthless... Okay, honey. We're gonna get you to the hospital. Do you think you can stand up for me?"

It's the hardest thing Paisley has ever done, but she gets up, trying as hard as she can not to move her left side. It hurts so much that it's hard to breathe, and that, more than anything, makes Paisley finally manage to stop crying.

"Please," Paisley gasps, "My clothes..."

The woman looks up at the teenager and nods.

The teenager starts picking up the shirts and pants, stuffing them all into the non-ripped bag as well as she can. Paisley, head pounding, limping badly, allows herself to be led by the woman toward her car.

As she lays down in the back seat, trying as hard as she can not to be sick again, she says a silent prayer of thanks that no one ever thought to go get Mickey.

1

ROURKE

My knock on the half-open hospital room door is met with a pissed-off grunt.

"Whaddya want?" a voice inside growls.

Turning to Mal, I grin. "Sounds like Bear's ready for visitors."

Mal smirks back. "Our little ray of sunshine."

I push the door open to find Bear sitting up in bed, looking angry as a grizzly. He's dressed in a hospital gown and has the blanket pulled up to his waist. His white hair is in disarray on top of his head, yanked out of its usual ponytail.

"Nice dress, darlin'," Mal comments, nodding at the gown as he steps into the room. "The blue really brings out the color of your eyes."

"You can fuck right off, you asshole," Bear mutters through his beard. "I ain't gonna be in this bed forever, and I'm still strong enough to kick your ass."

I can't help but burst out laughing. That just makes Bear angrier. "Sorry, brother," I say between chuckles. "I gotta go with Mal on this one. You look funny as hell in that get-up."

"Fuckin' assholes wouldn't let me keep my street clothes on," he grouses. "Said the blood on my shirt wasn't sterile, or some shit."

"How ya feelin', anyway?" Mal asks, leaning against the wall. "You lost a fuck of a lot of blood, brother."

"Eh, I'm okay." Bear brushes off the question with a frown. He shifts in the bed, wincing as he does. "They got me on some pain meds. Doc said it's gonna hurt like hell later."

"I don't doubt it," I agree. "But at least you got the satisfaction of knowing the other guy's probably in a lot more goddamn pain than you are."

It's true. The dumb fuck who made the mistake of putting his hands on Bear at the Viking Bar isn't likely to forget today anytime soon. The beatdown he got as a result is gonna leave some permanent damage to that guy's face. Not to mention, he's gonna be walking with a limp for a long, long time. Hell, if that limp-dick hadn't managed to pull a knife on Bear toward the end and stab him in the gut, they would have had to carry his ass out on a stretcher.

Bear shakes his head in disgust at the memory. "A fuckin' bar fight takes me down," he mutters. "I'm gettin' too old for this shit."

"You'll be up and fightin' again in no time, old man," Mal grins. "You still got it in ya. Granted," he concedes, "that beer gut you're sportin' helped cushion the blow a little..."

"Did you bring this motherfucker here to cheer me up?" Bear shoots at me. "Because he ain't cheerin' me up."

I don't answer that. "Hey," I say instead, "Axel says he's gonna be by later. He had some business to attend to."

"Ah..." Bear waves his giant, paw-like hand. "Tell the prez I'm fine. He doesn't need to do that." Bear is clearly embarrassed by all this attention. And by the fact that he's even here in the first place.

I open my mouth to answer him, but a sudden commotion from across the hall interrupts me. A female voice, pitched high with what sounds like fear, reaches my ears.

"Sir, you can't be here," the voice says frantically. "You're scaring her. Sir—"

"The fuck I can't!" explodes an angry male in response. "She ain't gotta be here. You already patched up her arm. Ain't no way she needs to be in that hospital bed. You're just tryin' to milk money outta her family."

I glance over at Mal with a frown. "Hold on a sec," I grunt to my two brothers. "Gonna go check this out."

The angry voices continue to ring out as I cross over to the room facing Bear's and stick my head through the doorway. Inside, a short, compact nurse is trying to prevent a steroid-jacked, aggressive-looking guy with a dark ponytail from grabbing at a tiny figure sitting on the hospital bed.

It's a little girl, who looks about six years old, with tangled hair and a cast on her arm. Her head is banged up, and her left eye's got a shiner. The girl is shrinking back against her pillows, clearly sick, and obviously scared. As the man and the nurse continue to argue, she draws her knees up against her chest in a defensive posture, hugging her legs tight to her torso.

"Hey," I bark out, causing all three of them to jump. "What's goin' on here?"

The nurse looks at me apprehensively. The guy arguing with her swivels toward me, his chest puffed out, chin jutting toward me. "You can fuck off, man. This ain't about you."

"You can keep that kinda language out of your mouth around the kid," I say, taking a step inside. "And I can hear your yellin' across the hall, which makes it my business."

"Her arm's just broke," the man snarls, nodding toward the kid. "Why she gotta be in the hospital for that? She got a cast, don't she?"

The nurse tries to speak calmly. "The child fell down a flight of stairs. She hit her head and has symptoms consistent with a moderate to severe concussion. We need to keep her here for observation, at least overnight."

I look down at the little girl. One thing is clear: she does not want to go with this guy. Everything about the way she's holding her body says she's afraid of him. Whoever the fuck he is, this situation ain't good.

"You her father?" I ask him.

He snorts. "Nah," he says dismissively. "She's my girlfriend's."

"Why ain't the mom here?"

"She's at work. Someone at the motel we're stayin' at told me the kid got hurt." His lip curls as he speaks. "I came down here to get her. Her mom don't need to get money taken outta her paycheck just 'cause her fuckin' kid's clumsy."

"I warned you about that language," I say, narrowing my eyes.

"If you aren't a relative of the girl's, you can't take her from the hospital without a parent or guardian's consent," the nurse insists.

"You heard the lady," I say, stepping between him and the bed. "You ain't got authorization. You need to leave."

"I ain't goin' anywhere," he retorts, his eyes flashing.

"I'm pretty sure you are."

The shit for brains takes a step toward me, not realizing that Mal has entered the room behind him. Mal grabs the fucker from behind just as I lean in and give him a solid punch to the gut. He buckles in half and as he does, my other fist meets his jaw in an uppercut. A resounding crack tells me the punch landed the way I wanted it to. His eyes roll back in his head as he slides to the ground.

That's all she wrote.

Placidly, Mal starts to drag him away. "Dump him in an elevator," I suggest. "Press the button for the first floor." I turn to the nurse. "You wanna call security to go get him?"

Mutely, she nods and rushes out of the room.

I don't bother to watch as Mal disappears with the now-unconscious asshole. Instead, I turn to the little girl, who is still sitting in the bed with her knees up protectively in front of her.

Her face is pale beneath the bruises around her eye and forehead. She looks exhausted. Her forehead is all scrunched up, like she's in pain.

There's something in her eyes, and her scrawny frame, that sends a sharp pierce of regret through my chest. A memory surfaces, from long ago.

A memory of my sister. How she used to look, back in the day. Before I could protect her.

My teeth clench. I wonder how much of why she's in this hospital bed is because of the piece of trash Mal just hauled out of here.

"That guy ain't very nice, is he?" I ask, trying hard as I can not to telegraph my anger through my voice.

The girl shakes her head, eyes wide as saucers.

I don't really know what else to say at this point, but one thing's for sure: I'm not about to leave her alone.

"So, what did you do to that arm?" I nod at the cast.

She swallows, and looks like she's trying to find her words. "I fell down the stairs," she finally says, her voice tiny and soft. "I was trying to take my clothes to the washing machine."

Huh. At first, I don't believe her. *I fell* is a pretty classic line that abused kids say. I should know. I used it myself, back in the day. But something in the way she says it makes me think she's telling the truth. At least about that part.

"Aren't you a little young to be doing laundry?"

"I'm seven," she pipes up, with just a degree of feistiness. Shit. She looks pretty small for a seven year-old.

"Oh," I say seriously. "My apologies."

"Is my mom gonna come soon?"

"Yeah. I'm sure she is."

I notice the girl seems to be untensing a little bit, so I move toward the foot of the bed and take a seat, far enough away from her that she'll have plenty of personal space. "So, what's your name?"

"Paisley," she mumbles, looking down at her cast.

"I'm Rourke. Pleased to meet you."

"Pleasetameetyoutoo."

The way she says it, like she's just remembering her manners, makes me chuckle.

"That guy's your mom's boyfriend, huh?" I ask her.

Paisley's eyes immediately grow dark and sad. "Yeah. His name is Mickey."

"You don't like him much, huh?"

"No..."

"Me neither."

Paisley risks a look at me. Her face looks like she's trying to figure out whether to say something. Finally, she does: "My mom says it's not okay to hit people."

"Your mom's right," I agree. "But..." I lean closer. "Can I tell you a secret?"

Paisley nods.

"Hitting him was fun."

Then, before my eyes, her face transforms. A tiny grin appears, which she lifts up her good hand to hide. She starts to giggle. Which makes me start to chuckle. Which makes her start full-on laughing.

It makes me happy as hell to hear her laugh, even though I can kind of tell it hurts her head to do it. Seems to me she probably hasn't done much laughing today.

I'm trying to think of something else I can do to cheer her up. Maybe the old "make a quarter appear behind her ear" trick or something. I'm casually reaching for my pocket to fish out a coin when a female voice behind me — different from the nurse's — rings out in the room.

"Excuse me!"

I frown at Paisley and shift on the foot of the bed to look toward the door.

A hot as hell woman with dark hair and flashing eyes stands

in the doorway, fists on her hips. She's dressed like she runs this place, in professional-looking navy-blue pants and a cream colored blouse that's unbuttoned to reveal the soft skin of her throat. The fabric swells to the curve of her breasts, which are rising and falling rapidly as she stares at me now, her brows arched in an unspoken challenge. Her lips are parted, plump, stained a berry-red that looks good enough to eat.

Or to wrap around my cock.

For a second, I forget everything about the situation and just kinda stare at her. *Holy hell.*

"Excuse me," she repeats — interrupting my budding fantasy of findin' an empty hospital bed somewhere to fuck her brains out. She glares at me, and then shoots a quick glance at Paisley before locking her eyes on me again. "Will you please tell me exactly what it is you're doing in this room?"

2

LANEY

I stare at the huge, scary-looking man defiantly, hoping I'm projecting a commanding presence I don't quite feel.

When Katie — my best friend and a nurse here at the hospital — called my office and told me there was a strange man in this room with the little girl, refusing to leave, I don't know exactly what I expected. But it sure as heck wasn't this. Sitting on the foot of the girl's bed is a man dressed all in denim and leather. He looks to be somewhere around thirty years old, with hard, rugged features roughly sculpted, almost as though from rock. His dark hair is cropped close, revealing high cheekbones, a strong, straight nose, and a square jaw accented by just a hint of shadow. Dark tattoos emerge from the collar of his black T-shirt and snake up his neck. The muscles in his arms, also tattooed, are hard and sculpted like the rest of him, making it difficult not to stare.

Even seated on the bed, the man is almost as tall as I am standing. Looking at him now, in the sterile environment of this hospital room, I somehow think of the proverbial bull in the china shop. He seems completely out of place, bursting with strength and energy that almost literally fills the room. He feels dangerous as a wild beast — a mountain I couldn't hope to move if I wanted to, no matter how hard I tried.

But even so. There is no way in hell I am going to let him do any harm this girl. Whoever he is, I am going to have to make him leave, no matter what it takes.

"I said, what are you doing in this room?" I demand. My voice comes out strong, thankfully — not betraying even a hint of fear. I know that if this man is dangerous, things could get bad here very quickly. I glance back toward the hallway, prepared to yell for security if I have to.

But instead of doing anything sudden or violent, the man gets leisurely to his feet, cocking a brow at me.

"What the f—..." he begins, then stops, with a glance toward the little girl. "What's your problem, lady?" he asks in a deep, rich baritone. "I'm just keeping Paisley here company. That ain't a crime, is it?"

"You're not a relative, and she is a minor," I retort. I step further into the room, realizing that if I'm trying to intimidate this man, I'm likely to fail miserably. If anything, he looks mildly amused, if not a little pissed off.

Mentally I kick myself that I didn't get here to see the girl earlier. About an hour ago, Katie came by my office and told me that a female minor had come here with a broken arm and a bad concussion — possibly malnourished, and needing a bath.

As the medical social worker on staff here at Morningside Hospital, it's my job to investigate situations like this — to determine whether there's any likelihood of physical abuse. But at the time, I was running behind on some paperwork, so I made a mental note to come see the little girl as soon as I finished. But then, just a few minutes ago, Katie called me again in a panic, saying there was a strange man here in her room, refusing to leave.

Maybe if I'd been here when he showed up, I could have

managed to keep him out of the girl's room in the first place. Now that he's in here, it's going to be a lot harder to get him out.

I take another step forward toward the bed. I'm about four feet away from the man now, and my God, he is *massive*. He stands almost a foot taller than I am, a wall of muscle wrapped in leather. His shoulders are almost broad enough to carry a sofa. His black vest and heavy boots mark him right off as a biker. Patches line the leather, indicating a sort of code I don't quite understand. But the tattooed mass of him — as well as the words "Lords of Carnage" and "Vice-President" over his pec — tell me he's definitely not a casual weekend rider.

As he towers over me, his eyes travel from my face to my neck, then down to my chest. He makes no secret of the fact that he's checking me out. He takes his sweet time about it, too. I feel my face flame, half from embarrassment and half from anger. *The nerve!* Thankfully, his back is to the little girl, so she can't see what he's doing.

The biker's eyes finally slide back up to lock on mine. As they do, corner of his mouth lifts, into just the hint of a lazy smirk. "What's the problem, darlin'?" he asks, his voice teasing, taunting. "You gonna toss me out on my ear?"

It's obvious he finds my attempts to intimidate him ridiculous. And of course, they are. I could throw my entire weight at him and probably not budge him an inch. If he doesn't want to leave, there's no way I can make him.

But, I have to admit that as dangerous as he seems, he doesn't really give off the vibe of a man who would hurt a child. I flick my eyes over to the little girl, who's watching both of us with more curiosity than anything. She doesn't seem at all afraid of him.

As a social worker, I know better than to put complete trust in appearances, of course. Some of the worst cases of abuse I've ever seen were at the hands of people you'd never imagine capable of it. But this doesn't feel at all like the situation I thought I'd be stepping into when Katie called me.

"I'm sorry, but you'll have to leave," I say uncertainly, all the strength in my voice seeming to have left me.

"Uh-uh," he rumbles, taking a step closer. His dark eyes seem to see right through me, making me feel strangely exposed. "But hey, darlin', if you wanna try to make me, be my guest," he says, his voice dropping until only I can hear what he's saying. "Might be fun."

Alarm bells start to go off somewhere deep in the back of my brain. But now, they aren't because I'm afraid he's going to hurt the little girl in that bed.

They're going off because of the way he's looking at me. Like he can see right through the professional air I'm struggling to maintain with him.

Like maybe he can tell I'm trying not to notice how handsome he is. How sexy and raw.

Maybe he can tell I'm trying not to think about what a man like him would be like in bed.

What it would be like to let him take control. Whether he'd be rough.

Whether I'd like it.

Involuntarily, a small sound escapes my throat.

The biker hears it.

The corner of his mouth quirks up a little more.

Oh my God. I feel the heat rush to my cheeks. I am rapidly losing what little control I have of this situation.

"It's inappropriate for an unknown adult male to be in this room," I tell him in a strangled tone.

He pauses a beat, considering me. The expression on his face gives me the distinct impression he's disappointed in me.

"What's inappropriate is for the kid to be alone in this room without protection," he says flatly. "Look, Paisley's mom's not here yet. And I'm stickin' around until she does get here. Period."

"I can't leave her in here alone with a stranger," I insist. "It's this hospital's job to make sure she's safe and not in any danger."

"Lady, if that's the case, this hospital is doin' a piss poor job of it." Irritated, he glances over at the girl before continuing. "Look, let's take this out in the hall. Paisley, you good here?"

To my surprise, the girl immediately nods, looking at him trustingly. Before I can make sense of it all, I find myself following him out into the hallway.

I'm giving this man way more power in this conversation than I intended to. *Dammit.*

"Who are you, anyway?" he demands as soon as we're out of the room, nodding at my outfit. "Some bureaucrat?"

"I'm a social worker," I say defensively. "In other words, an employee of this hospital. I think the real question is, who are *you*?"

"I'm visiting someone in that room there," he says, jerking his thumb across the hall. "I heard a commotion over here and came in to find some scumbag yellin' at a nurse and scaring the kid."

My brain works to make sense of what he's saying. The nurse he's talking about must be Katie, of course. When I got the frantic call from her a few minutes ago, she said a strange man was in the girl's room and refusing to leave. I just assumed *this* was the man. But now, I'm not so sure.

"You... came over here trying to get *another* man to leave?" I ask stupidly.

"Not *tryin'*. I got him out of here. Look," he mutters, glancing at the closed door of Paisley's room. "I just got rid of the only danger that kid was in. Her mom's scumbag boyfriend was in there yellin' about how he was gonna take her out of here and no one could stop him." He crosses his arms in front of him and cocks his head. "Well, I stopped him."

"So..." I say in confusion, "you *aren't* the man the nurse called about?"

"Jesus Christ," he growls, raking a massive hand through his hair. "Are you listening at all? For the last time, *no*. Though I don't think that nurse was much of a fan of me either."

Just then, hurried steps draw both of our attention down the hallway. Katie is striding toward us, followed by a harried-looking woman in heels and a faded denim mini-skirt. She's a bleached blond, her hair so light it's almost white, but it's been a while since she's had her it treated. Her roots are the same color as the little girl's hair.

"Where's my daughter?" the woman cries.

Katie stops in front of us. "Laney, this is Paisley's mom." To the woman, she says, "Your daughter is in there," and points to the door.

"So that's the scumbag's girlfriend," the biker mutters after the mother has hurried into the room. "How the hell do women fall for lowlifes like that?" He looks disgusted.

Katie looks at me and rolls her eyes. The biker catches the look and snorts.

"For fuck's sake," he mutters, turning away from both of us. "You're welcome, by the way."

Before either Katie or I can react, the biker sticks his head through the doorway to the little girl's room. "Yo, Paisley! I told you your mom would be here soon!"

Through the opening, I see the mother perched beside her on the bed. The girl turns and gives him a wide, beaming smile. "Thanks, Rourke!"

"No problem. I'll catch you later, little one. Okay?"

"Okay!"

He pulls back from the door and gives us both an angry look. "Keep an eye on her, for fuck's sake. That scumbag boyfriend of her mom's is no good."

Then he turns to me. He scans my face, eyes lingering for a long moment.

Somehow, my insides feel like they're turning into molten liquid.

"See you around, Laney the social worker," he murmurs.

I can actually feel my heart thudding inside my chest as I

watch him turn on his heel and go back into the room across from Paisley's.

Beside me, Katie blows out a breath.

"Whoa. He's hot," she exhales. "But scary. I can't believe *he* was calling the mom's boyfriend a scumbag. I mean, hello? Pot, meet kettle!"

Before I realize my mouth is even open, I hear myself snap: "Just because he rides a motorcycle doesn't make him a scumbag, Katie."

Katie shoots me a surprised look. "Wow. Okay, sorry. You're actually defending him?"

"Well, he protected that little girl, after all," I retort. "Didn't he?"

"I mean, yeah, I guess," she concedes, clearly not happy about it. "But who's to say he isn't some sort of weird perv or something himself?"

I shake my head in disbelief. "That's... just silly, Kate. Why would you think that?"

"Um, maybe because he looks like a total criminal?" She wrinkles her nose. "What is up with you? Are you into him, or something?"

"No. *God*, no." I laugh weakly. "I just think he, you know, deserves some credit for what he did. Don't you? Besides, if you were that worried about him, why did you leave the little girl alone with him?"

That shuts her up for a moment. "I went to get security," she fires back finally. "So yeah, I thought the boyfriend was the bigger problem. That doesn't mean I thought the biker guy was *safe*."

I open my mouth to protest some more, but then close it again. Why am I insisting on this? Why am I so irritated that she's judging him? After all, just a couple of minutes ago, I was basically doing the same thing.

"Okay, fine," I say irritably. "Let's just forget it. It's over now. Come on, let's go in and talk to the mom."

"Fine," Katie mutters back. She does a barely perceptible eye roll that I catch but decide to ignore. Suppressing a sigh, I let her open the door to Paisley's room and fall in behind her.

Katie's words echo in my head as I follow her inside:

He's hot, but scary.

It's true, there's something about him that's definitely a little frightening.

But what's scaring me has less to do with the possibility that he might be a criminal.

And everything to do with the fact that when he looked into my eyes, for just a moment I might have done almost anything he asked me to.

3

ROURKE

"How's Bear?" Axel asks as I climb off my bike in front of the clubhouse.

I came directly here from the hospital. My prez is standing next to his own motorcycle, having a smoke.

"He's fine," I say. "Grumpy as all fuck, but he'll live." Grabbing my own pack, I fish out a cigarette and light one up to keep him company. "How's Dos Santos?"

"Chaco had a little run-in with the law, he tells me," Axel grunts, referring to the head of the Dos Santos cartel. "Local cops came sniffing around, looking for evidence of criminal activity. Luckily Chaco's men managed to move the product to another location before the law arrived to check things out. But Chaco's sayin' they're gonna need to lay low for a bit until the heat's off them."

The Dos Santos cartel is our main supplier of drug shipments from the south. Our relationship with them is crucial to keeping the pipeline open to the north, toward our charter club of the Lords of Carnage in Tanner Springs. Angel, the prez of the main charter, is looking to expand our business, but we can't do that unless we have a steady and reliable supply of product.

If Dos Santos loses its grip on their territory, that puts all our plans in jeopardy. I know Axel is thinking the same thing.

"That ain't good." I take a drag on my smoke. "We gonna have a problem gettin' shipments from them?"

"Chaco assures me we won't," Axel mutters, but he looks dubious.

"He have any idea how the cops got tipped off?"

"He said he didn't. But I dunno. The fuckin' turf wars between the cartels have been heating up down there. Seem unlikely the cops found out by themselves. Chaco's been running that part of the pipeline for a while now, and he's careful." Axel blows out a breath. "We can't rule out the possibility that one of the other groups is tryin' to destroy the Dos Santos cartel by feeding info to the law about them."

I nod. "Or that the local cops are in cahoots with one of them."

"Yeah." Axel's face is stony. "Let's not get too worried yet, but we gotta keep our eyes open on this."

We finish our smokes and head inside. It's late afternoon, and after the last couple hours, I'm in the mood for a beer. There's no bartender behind the bar right now, so I go back and grab myself a bottle, then sink onto a stool and take a long swig. Axel, still looking preoccupied, gives me a quick chin lift and heads into the back.

The clubhouse is pretty deserted. In an hour or two, things will start to heat up, as they usually do. But for now, the only other brothers here are Rogue and Yoda, who are playing pool at the table in the center of the room.

Silently, I watch them play and give each other shit as my mind wanders back to the hospital. I'm still thinking about the little kid, her mom, and that asshole boyfriend of hers. At the time, I didn't think too much further than getting the boyfriend out of the room so he wouldn't be agitating Paisley. But now, as I sit and nurse my beer, I start to get a bad feeling about that whole situation.

The mom's boyfriend's name is Mickey, Paisley said. I haven't seen him around town, but he looks like a lowlife, for sure. I should have stuck around at the hospital a little longer, tried to find out more about the guy. What his last name is, what his story is. If he lives with the mom and the kid. And if so, where.

"Hey, Yoda," I call out.

Over at the pool table, he takes his shot, then lifts his head and turns toward me. "Yeah."

"Need you to get some intel on a guy in town."

"Okay. What's the name?"

"All I got is his first name. Mickey. Had a run-in with him earlier at the hospital. His girlfriend's kid is in the room across the hall. The guy's a real piece of shit."

"That ain't a lot to go on." Yoda leans his pool cue against the table and comes over to talk to me. "You got anything else?"

"I can describe him to you." I give him the guy's approximate height, weight, his hair and eye color. "He's got tattoos on his fingers. The four card suits on his left, and that EWMN thing on the right." I suppress a snort. *Evil, wicked, mean and nasty*, my ass. "Except the pinky of his right hand is gone, so it's just WMN."

"Good eye. Anything else?"

"Not about him specifically. Like I said, it's his girlfriend's kid who's in the room across the hall from Bear. Kid's name's Paisley. I think they're stayin' at one of the motels in town, but I don't know which one."

Yoda thinks for a moment. "I can find out the kid's last name, since she'd be registered at the hospital. There ain't that many motels in Ironwood. I can check around and figure out where they're at. Shouldn't be too hard from there to find out who this Mickey guy is."

I nod. "Good. I wanna know who he runs with. I wanna keep an eye on this son of a bitch. He gives me a bad feeling."

There's no way this guy's any danger to me, or my club. I can tell just by lookin' at him he's too small-time for that. But I don't like that he's around Paisley and her mom.

"Sure thing," Yoda agrees. "I'm goin' over to see Bear in a bit anyway. I'll do some snooping around at the hospital while I'm there. I'll chat up one of the nurses or somethin' if I have to."

I snort. Yoda's an ugly-ass motherfucker, but damned if he doesn't know how to charm the pants off of women. I don't know how the hell he does it.

"Thanks, brother." I clap him on the back. "Let me know what you find out."

"Will do."

"Hey, princess," Rogue calls to Yoda from across the room. "You ever gonna finish this game?"

"You want that cue up your ass, motherfucker?" Yoda tosses back easily.

I turn back to my beer, listening with half an ear. The clack of the billiard balls fades into the background as I wonder what Yoda will discover for me.

I'm pretty sure that Mickey dude ain't gonna turn out to be a pillar of the goddamn community. Whatever bullshit he's involved in, I hope it doesn't end up hurting Paisley.

My mind replays the scene of Paisley's mom rushing down the hallway to see her daughter. She seemed to care about the kid, at least. Although if Paisley was telling the truth, it's kind of fucked up that her mom left a seven year-old all alone in their motel room with an asshole like Mickey.

I frown and shake my head, taking a swig of my beer. Even though Mal and I got that piece of garbage out of Paisley's room earlier, that ain't no guarantee he won't be back. At least the hot social worker seems like she was trying to keep the kid safe. Though in my experience, social workers end up doin' more harm than good a lot of the time.

I let out a breath and shake my head at the memory of her.

She sure as hell ain't like any other social worker I've ever seen. For one thing, she carries herself like she comes from money. For another, she's sexy as all get-out. A real stunner. The flash in those amber-green eyes of hers as she argued with me back there? Hell, it went straight to my dick.

I wouldn't mind sparring with her some more. In the bedroom, that is.

Something tells me if I could get her to loosen up, she'd be one hell of a ride.

Now that's a challenge I wouldn't mind taking on.

I'M FIGHTING to keep my cock from going to full mast when I hear the scrape of a stool beside me. I turn to see Gage lift his chin as he sits down next to me at the bar.

"Whaddya know, brother?" he asks.

"Not much. Just sittin' here waitin' for the party to start," I smirk. "You wanna grab a bottle of Jack and start it ourselves?"

Gage grimaces. "Can't, brother," he mutters regretfully. "I gotta get home in a bit. I gotta go to a fuckin' school play, if you can believe that shit."

I laugh out loud. "What the fuck? You're shittin' me."

"I wish I was," he grunts. "They're puttin' on The Wizard of goddamn Oz over at Bailey and Addi's school." Gage shakes his head slowly. "Twenty third graders, doin' a full-blown musical. Jesus. Addi's playin' the cowardly lion. Fuckin' shoot me now."

"I'm tempted, man," I joke. "Someone needs to put you out of your misery."

Gage lowers the cigarette and blows out a puff of smoke. "You got that right," he half-chuckles. "Anyway, tonight's opening night, and Bailey says Addi is shittin' a brick. So, I gotta go tell her she's the next Meryl Streep afterwards."

Gage makes a big show out of being disgusted at the whole thing. But I know better. Ever since he met that hot elementary school teacher Bailey, he's turned into a consummate family man. Gage is fuckin' gone over that woman. And over Bailey's kid Addi, too. It doesn't take a genius to see that Gage loves that little girl like she's his own.

So, even though I'm pretty sure spending two hours in a folding chair watching little kids run around and pretend they're in the Wonderful Land of Oz ain't exactly his idea of a great time, I also know he wouldn't miss that shit for the world.

As I listen to Gage put on an award-winning performance of his own about how much he's gonna hate the whole thing, I suppress a grin. Whoever would've thought that Gage, of all people, would get lassoed by a chick with a kid? All I can say is, Bailey must have a golden pussy to have roped him so completely.

But even so, I have to admit she's an okay chick. She loves Gage to the ends of the goddamn earth, that much is obvious. And as far as I can tell, the feeling's mutual.

Yeah, the thing between Gage and Bailey is real. It's solid.

And in my experience, that's rare as shit.

Which is why I've avoided gettin' involved with women like the plague. From what I've seen, most of the time it just ain't worth the hassle. Hell, pussy's easy enough to come by. No reason to get all desperate and hand your balls over in a paper bag. Even if, like I said, Gage seems happier than he's ever been.

Gage is one of the lucky ones. The rest of us aren't likely to be the same.

Gage takes off for home. I grab another beer, and a bunch of brothers and a few club girls start streaming in. The music gets cranked, and I see beginnings of a party that will probably go late into the night.

For some reason, I find my thoughts turning to the hot social worker chick again more than once as the liquor starts to flow.

Laney. That's what the uptight nurse called her.

I look at my phone and check the time. Visiting hours are over by now.

I wonder how Paisley's doing. And if Mickey ever came back.

Almost without thinking about it, I decide I'm gonna go over to the hospital tomorrow morning, and check on the situation.

Just in case.

4

LANEY

Work gets pretty busy after my run-in with the biker. I get called away to talk to the family of a patient who's transitioning to hospice care for stage four cancer. Then after that, I help with planning a move to a drug treatment facility for a patient who was brought in after an overdose.

For a few hours, the little girl with the concussion and the broken arm moves to the back of my mind.

But as I'm leaving the hospital later — at least an hour after I was supposed to be off the clock — Paisley's pale little face comes back to me. I meant to check back at her room before I left, but I'm already in my car and halfway home before I remember.

The truth is, I'm worried about the girl. The fact that she was unsupervised when her accident happened concerns me. Her mom did seem embarrassed about it — though she claims the boyfriend was home, just not paying attention. In the end, I'm not sure what to think about the whole thing.

THE MOM — who gave her name as Bethany Hawn — reacted with shock when we told her Paisley had been lugging a load of laundry down the stairs when she fell. "I told you never to leave the room when we're gone!" she hissed at the little girl, before catching herself and looking at me guiltily. As though she could sense that her fitness as a mother might be on the line here.

"I know," Paisley mumbled back, staring down at the bedspread. "But Mickey was there. And Callista said I smelled."

"Who's..." Bethany started, then went silent. Swallowing, her voice shook a little when she continued. "I'm sorry, baby," she half-whispered. "Money's a little tight right now." She leaned forward and gathered the little girl in her arms. Paisley visibly relaxed, sinking into her with the ultimate trust of a child toward a loving parent.

Then Bethany turned to me. Her eyes were red-rimmed and wide.

"I'm not a bad mother, I swear," she pleaded.

In her eyes was a fear I know only too well. I've seen it before. On the faces of the poor, who know that their actions are scrutinized more closely by people like me than others with more money. Rich people have more cash to throw at their problems, and to dress up their faults and their mistakes.

Everything tells me that this mother loves her child. And that the child loves her. I don't see abuse or neglect there. Just struggle against a world that gave them the short end of the stick. I've been wrong before, but I've seen enough to at least partially trust my gut.

However, I'm worried that's not the whole story.

In talking with Doctor Methaney, the doctor who examined Paisley, he told me he noticed a bruise forming on Paisley's upper arm, consistent with being grabbed roughly. He said it looked like a larger size hand. And that, of course, makes me think of one thing.

The boyfriend.

I know I need to talk to Paisley's mom about this. But I also want to try as hard as I can to make sure she trusts me first.

Paisley's safe in the hospital for now, I reason as I pull up in front of the tiny house I rent on the north side of town. *I'll go talk to Bethany some more tomorrow.*

THE SUN IS JUST STARTING to set as I emerge from my car. Keys in hand, I'm walking toward my front door when my phone buzzes in my purse. I reach inside and glance at the screen.

It's my own mother. What a coincidence.

Groaning, I purse my lips and decide to answer it. If I don't, it's just prolonging the inevitable — and probably earning myself a passive-aggressive voice message in the process.

"Hi, Mom!" I say brightly. "What's up?"

There's a short pause. "Well, I'm fine, Delaney, thank you for asking. How are you?"

Ugh. And so it begins. "I'm sorry, Mom," I say, gritting my teeth. "How are you?"

"As I said, I'm fine." God, she can pack *so* much judgment into just a few words. It really is a talent.

"I'm glad to hear it," I reply, trying as hard as I can not to be snippy back to her. "I'm doing well, also."

There's a pregnant silence on the line for a few seconds. I open my mouth to try to fill it, but then the stubborn part of me takes control. If I ask her why she's calling again, we'll just be back at square one. I know that sometimes with my mom, there's just no winning. This already feels like one of these times. So, my basic strategy is to just try not to play the game at all.

"Your father's fine, too, by the way," she finally sniffs.

"I'm so glad to hear it!" I enthuse, refusing to rise to the bait. By now, I'm at my front stoop. Instead of going inside my house right away, I decide to sit down on the top step. "Tell me more. What have you two been up to?"

Grudgingly, she launches into a narrative that's still tinged with an *as though you care* tone. But if there's one thing my mother loves doing, it's talking about herself, so I know this is the quickest way to defuse her temper. Sure enough, within a couple of minutes she's caught up in some story of how their friends the Meads are splitting up after twenty-nine years of marriage, and *isn't that just terrible.* (Of course, the barely-suppressed cattiness in my mom's voice tells me that she is thoroughly enjoying the scandal — after all, marital strife is great fodder for society gossip among the wealthy.)

"I do have a wonderful bit of news," she finally says, switching gears.

Aha. This must be the main reason she's calling. "What's that?" I ask.

"Lindsay is engaged!"

"Oh, that's nice," I murmur. "Who to?"

"Oh, for God's sake, Delaney," my mother huffs. "To Nick, of course. We're just all so happy. Of course, your father is over the moon."

Yeah. He would be. Robert Harris, Nick's father, is my dad's biggest donor. The Harris family of Louisville is one of the richest in the state. Marriage to their only son is a fantastic alliance for a senator's daughter. My younger sister couldn't possibly have made a better match, as far as my parents are concerned.

Even though Nick Harris is a self-important, moneyed asshole who doesn't give two shits about her, beyond the fact that she's arm candy and a senator's daughter.

And this, of course, is the subtle dig, and the *real* reason my mother is calling — unsaid, but coming through as clear as a bell.

My sister is fulfilling her destiny as the daughter of a prominent politician. She fully embraces her trophy wife future of shopping trips, charity balls, personal trainers, and spa dates.

I, on the other hand, insist on slumming it as a soon-to-be-old maid social worker out in the middle of nowhere, southern Ohio.

My mother chatters on blissfully about how Nick proposed (a ring brought on a silver platter at dessert at the most expensive restaurant in town, how original), how Lindsay has already booked the wedding venue, and who will do their engagement photos. There's a mention of Lindsay's maid of honor, as well.

Which is when I realize that Lindsay herself hasn't called me about any of this.

I'm guessing I will not be asked to be one of the bridesmaids. I should probably feel bad about that, but instead, I feel an immediate sense of relief. The only thing I can imagine more uncomfortable than attending this high-profile wedding is having to stand in front of the five-hundred or so guests that will no doubt be there during the ceremony, enduring their scrutiny and their whispered comments about the *still single older sister*. All while wearing an uncomfortable, frou frou dress that I'll need assistance to take on and off.

Finally, my mom's excitement starts to wind down after she's told me literally every single detail she can think of. "Well," she eventually sighs, her tone shifting. "So, what's new with you, Delaney?"

She sounds so resigned I almost laugh. Neither one of my parents has approved of a single decision I've made since I switched my major in college from English to social work. They tried everything they could think of to try to get me to change my mind, including my father threatening to cut off my college funding. (He eventually backed down on that, probably reasoning that a daughter who was a college dropout was an even worse look for him than a daughter who was majoring in something so pedestrian.)

After graduation, my parents leaned on me hard to channel the social work degree into working for one of the prestigious nonprofits in Louisville — that is, one of the organizations where young socialites could spend time working for a socially-acceptable "cause" while looking for their future husbands.

But by that time, I had been away from home long enough to know that the very last thing in the world I wanted to do with my life was follow in the footsteps of my parents.

Not their socialite lifestyle. And *especially* not their marriage.

My mother, for all her surface haughtiness and impeccable pedigree in tony Louisville society, is in actuality one of the most miserable people I've ever met. And the strange thing is, I'm not even sure she realizes it. Underneath the shiny surface of being Senator Rodney Hart's lovely wife, the fact is that she lives under the thumb of a bully who scrutinizes and criticizes her every thought, word, and deed. And always has.

And somehow, my mother thinks it should be my life's aspiration to be just like her.

When I got this job in Ironwood, it caused a family scandal so large, you would have thought I'd revealed I was addicted to crack.

The fact that I've *kept* this job? And that it's become clear to my parents this isn't just some youthful rebellion?

Well, let's just say that one of the advantages is that they hardly ever talk about me anymore in their social circles.

It's sort of a relief being a pariah, to be honest. There's a lot less pressure. When I go home to visit, they're a lot less likely to parade me around in all the hot spots of Louisville. I'm an embarrassment to them. And I'll continue to be, until I reform myself, realize the error of my ways, and come crawling back into the fold.

So even though most daughters in my situation might tell their mothers all about what happened at work today -- that I met a little girl and a mom, and I'm worried about them — I find myself swallowing back the words.

"Oh, you know," I chirp instead. "Same old, same old."

"Yes, well," Mom replies drily. "You know I just don't understand why you insist on doing a job like that, Delaney. It's certainly not like you *have* to work. And the pay can't be all that much after all. It's just incomprehensible to me."

I roll my eyes as I stand up from the stoop and slip my key into the lock of my front door. This conversation happens in one form or another practically every time I talk to my mother. Mom's attitude toward social work is basically, *These things happen to other people, it's not our issue.*

Whereas I know otherwise, from experience. The rich have the same problems as everyone else. They just have enough money to pretend like they don't.

"Okay, Mom," I mutter, entering my house and tossing my purse on a chair. "Look, I'm just on my way somewhere, so I'm gonna have to let you go. Okay? Talk soon."

Mom huffs again, but doesn't put up much of an argument. After all, the point of this conversation was never to actually talk to *me.*

"Alright, darling. I assume we'll see you next month for your father's birthday?"

"I wouldn't miss it," I say through gritted teeth.

The phone goes dead. I shake my head and sigh.

At least my mom only calls a couple of times a month.

Moving into my bedroom, I change out of my work clothes and put on a loose T-shirt and a pair of yoga pants. Slipping my feet into a favorite pair of flip-flops, I go into the kitchen and try to figure out something quick to make for dinner. I settle on an omelet with ham and cheddar, which I eat sitting on the couch.

Out of curiosity, I grab my phone from the cushion where I've tossed it and open up Instagram. A few seconds later, I'm staring at a picture of Lindsay's engagement ring, in close-up, adorning a carefully manicured hand.

#engaged #mrsharris #whyyesthatismyring #junewedding

MY SISTER LINDSAY. The modern socialite/influencer. The daughter who *is* following in her mother's footsteps.

I'm happy for her. Sort of.

But God, I'm glad I'm not her.

I SPEND the next couple of hours binge-watching bad TV shows, feeling exhausted and drained by work and by the conversation with my mother. Usually, watching *Brooklyn-Nine-Nine* is silly and funny enough to take my mind off the day, but tonight it's not working.

As the evening wears on, I find my thoughts drifting away from little Paisley, away from my sister. And toward the gruff biker I met in Paisley's hospital room.

He's hot. But scary.

He's hot, all right. Embarrassingly so. Especially because now that I'm home alone, with nothing but the memory of the way his eyes slid over my body, I find myself wondering again what his touch would feel like.

I bet his hands would be rough.

I bet the calluses would make me tremble as they traveled over my skin.

I bet sex with him would be rough, and raw, and...

Amazing.

As my eyes continue to stare at the screen, my mind is now a million miles away. With the hot biker, peeling off my clothes. Sliding me underneath him. Pushing himself inside me. My skin tingles. Between my legs, heat pools, my panties soaking wet. My nipples grow taut, crying out for his touch.

Before I know it, I've turned off the TV and gone into my

bedroom. I push off my yoga pants, peel off my top, and slip beneath the covers.

And there, in the dark, my fingers find my hot, waiting sex. Barely a minute later, I'm coming, shuddering through my orgasm and whispering the name of a man I don't even know.

Rourke.

5

ROURKE

The next day, I'm at the hospital before nine, with the excuse of visiting Bear again.

When I get up to the floor where his room is, Paisley's door is closed. I stand in the hall for a second, listening, but it's pretty quiet inside. That's probably a good thing, unless they've moved her to a different room.

I find Bear still living up to his name. It wouldn't take a genius to predict a guy like him would be a bad patient. Of course, I'd probably be the same way in his situation. He's still mad as hell about being cooped up in this place. From the looks of him, he's feeling a lot better this morning — but that just gives him more energy to bitch and moan about everything.

"I'm fine," he's barking at the nurse who's hovering around him, trying to adjust his bed. I recognize her as the same one from yesterday — the one who was tryin' to get that jackass out of Paisley's room. She looks up as I come in, and raises her eyebrows briefly in recognition.

"Your friend here doesn't seem to be enjoying his stay with us," she tells me.

I laugh. "Yeah, I coulda predicted that. Bear, why don't you lay off the nurse? She's just tryin' to do her job."

"I don't need her to do her job. I need her to leave me the hell alone."

"The sooner you get better, the sooner you can get out of here," I counter. "She's trying to help you get better." I snicker. "I'm pretty sure she probably wants you outta here as much as *you* want you outta here."

"You got that right," she mutters under her breath.

The nurse, who's got a name tag that reads *Katie*, continues to bustle around, looking at monitors and shit. I figure I'll do my part, so I try to keep Bear occupied with conversation. Pretty soon, she leaves, and I settle into one of the crappy chairs sitting over by the window.

"Axel ever stop by last night?" I ask.

"Yep." Bear nods. "He was here for a while. There was a pretty steady stream of brothers for most of the day." He snorts, then winces a little. "Barely had a moment to myself. I don't know why you fuckers think you need to babysit me here."

"Most of 'em probably were hopin' to see you on your death bed," I joke. "Now that they know you'll probably recover, I imagine they're so disappointed they won't be back."

"Har, har."

Heavy steps resound in the hallway. A second later, Axel walks in, followed by Mal, our Sergeant at Arms, and Dante, our Enforcer.

"Ah, geez," Bear groans. "Here we go again."

"Bear seems to be less than appreciative of our company," I explain.

"Oh yeah?" Mal grins. "Good. Nothing makes me happier than pissin' off Bear. Speakin' of which, we brought you something."

"Yeah?" Bear sneers. "What's that?"

With a smirk, Mal steps outside for a second. When he comes

back, he's carrying a floral arrangement of white daisies and pink carnations in a blue container. Stuck into the arrangement is a balloon on a stick that says "Feel better soon!" and a little stuffed bear hanging onto the stick.

I start laughing so fuckin' hard I think they're gonna have to hospitalize *me*.

"Jesus fuckin' Christ," Bear mutters. "I gotta get the hell outta here."

My brothers keep up a pretty good pace of harassing Bear out of his bad mood. I take the opportunity to slip out and see if I can check in on Paisley, but when I go out into the hallway, her door's still closed. Shrugging, I figure I'll go take a walk downstairs and grab myself a smoke.

I stay outside for a while, enjoying the fresh air in between cigarettes. Jesus, I hate hospitals. I suppose most people do. The smells get to me, and the cold, impersonal feel of them. All the people inside, living their own personal dramas. So much sickness, and death, and worry.

I could never understand why someone would choose to work in a place like that. I have a harder time than most being cooped up inside. I need my freedom, and the outdoors, and the open road. Spending all day in a giant, fluorescent-lit box seems like my own personal version of hell. The only way I can handle bein' inside this place is because I ain't a patient. I can leave any time I want.

As I smoke, my mind goes back to Laney the social worker, who I imagine is inside somewhere. I wonder where she comes from originally. She sure as shit didn't grow up around here. No way a chick that hot would have been off my radar.

It occurs to me again how much she doesn't look like any kind of social worker I've ever seen. The way she walks into a room, it's like she owns the place. She doesn't seem scared of anything, or anyone. That's the kind of confidence that comes from money. From never thinking about what your place is in the world. Never worrying where your next meal is coming from. Never worrying whether your mom and dad can make rent.

I roll around the question of Laney in my head some more while I finish my second smoke. I'm not in the mood to go back up to Bear's room yet, but there's nothing to see out here except some sad-ass potted shrubs and a parking lot. I go back inside and take a walk around the first floor of the hospital, just to kill some time before heading back upstairs. I pass by the gift shop where Mal must have got Bear's potted plant with the balloon and the stuffed bear. Further down is a cafeteria, which smells exactly like you'd expect a hospital cafeteria to smell. There's a coffee shop, too, which is good to know in case I ever want something stronger than piss water.

I reach the end of that hallway, backtrack to the entrance, and then start down the other hall to the right. I make it about halfway down to the end, when I see a familiar figure fiddling with the knob on a locked door about twenty feet in front of me.

"What the fuck are you doin' here?" I bite out at Mickey when he's close enough to notice me walking toward him. His expression contorts in anger. I notice with satisfaction that the entire left side of his face is bruised a dark purple.

"I'm visiting my girlfriend's kid," he snarls. "You ain't got nothin' to say about it, either." He pauses, then puffs up his gym rat pecs. "I could call the cops on you, man. Get your ass thrown in jail for hittin' me yesterday."

I let out a bark of laughter. "Are you fuckin' kidding me, you piece of shit? You've got shithole thug written all over your face. I bet you got a list of stupid-ass petty crimes a mile long." I lift my chin at the ugly-ass scruff of facial hair he's sporting. "That prison pussy would probably come to good use in county. You ever been anybody's bitch, junior?"

For a second I think he's gonna launch himself at me. Which I would fuckin' *love*. His hands curl into fists, his body posture shifting like he's getting ready to charge, but then he seems to think better of it.

"Fuck you, asshole," he hisses.

"Great comeback, dipshit."

Mickey gives me the double-barrel middle finger and brushes past me, just narrowly avoiding knocking into me with his shoulder.

I bust out laughing again and head toward the first floor nurses' station about fifteen feet down the hallway.

"Hey, can I ask you something?" I say to a slim redheaded nurse sitting behind the desk. She's typing on a computer, and when she looks up at me she does a double-take.

"Um, yes, what is it?" she asks, a little breathlessly.

I turn and glance down the hall at Dipshit, who's just disappearing out the front door. "What are the rules for who can and can't visit a patient here? Especially a little kid?"

The nurse frowns a little, looking confused. "As long as the parent is okay with the person visiting the child, we have no restrictions," she half shrugs. "Why?"

"No reason," I growl, turning away. "Thanks."

I take the stairs up to the second floor, and head toward Paisley's room, pissed. That fuckin' sleazebag should not be around this kid, I'm sure of it.

And I'm gonna do something about it. One way or another.

I'm just about to knock on the door to Paisley's room when I hear the clicking of high heels on the vinyl floor. I look toward the sound. Laney, the hot social worker chick, is just rounding the corner, her head bent toward a clipboard she's holding.

"Hey!" I yell, turning on my heel. "I need to talk to you."

She looks up, startled. When she sees me storming down the hall, instead of looking afraid or intimidated, she just lowers the clipboard and squares her stance. She tosses her head just slightly, sending her cascade of dark hair over one shoulder.

"Can I help you?" she asks mildly.

She's a cool one, this social worker. She's got this classy ice-queen thing going on. This *you aren't good enough for me* attitude that half makes me mad, and half turns me on.

She's wearing glasses today. Hot librarian horn-rimmed glasses.

Makes me want to get a library card. And fuck her in the stacks.

My cock springs to attention before I even realize it's happening.

Fuck. Pull your shit together, Rourke.

"Why the fuck did I just see that kid's mom's boyfriend in here just now?" I demand, trying to ignore the rush of blood to my cock. "Isn't anybody watching out for her?"

Laney's gaze flickers, and she draws in a breath. "I'm sorry, but the hospital can't guard every patient staying here," she says, sounding a little impatient.

"That's bullshit. The second you saw me in Paisley's room yesterday, you tried to get me out of there."

"That's not the same," she protests. "You have no connection to her. You were a total stranger, and we hadn't yet located the mother. And quite frankly," she adds, tossing a glance at my cut and tattoos, "between him and you, you look quite a bit more dangerous on the face of it."

She's looking at me with this expression I can't quite read. On the one hand, she's clearly trying to pull rank on me. On the other hand, her green eyes are dilated as hell right now. And her breathing is speeding up. I can tell because her tits are rising and falling faster under that pale pink blouse she's wearing, distracting the shit out of me.

Well, well, well. Miss stuck-up social worker is hot for me.

I suppress a grin.

"Yeah. I'm dangerous," I agree with a smirk. "But not to a kid, for fuck's sake. That guy, though... he's bad news. You can't tell me you don't see that!"

"Are you suggesting that I should judge people based on appearances?" she smirks back, cocking her head at me.

"No, on his actions," I counter. "Are you forgetting I got that guy out of here yesterday? Paisley didn't want him here. She told me."

She blinks up at me, surprised. "She said that?"

I nod. "As good as. She said she didn't like him. She was scared as shit of him. You didn't see the way she reacted — pulling her legs up in front of her, like she was trying to protect herself. She was pretty happy I got rid of him." I shake my head. "Fuck. You tried to get me away from that kid, when I was protecting her, but you let that asshole come and go as he pleases."

She looks troubled, uncertain. "He is her mother's boyfriend," she murmurs, frowning. "She's authorized him to be here. And there's no reason to think the little girl is in any immediate danger from him while she's here in the hospital."

"You're full of shit," I scoff. "You can't think it's good for her to be around him?"

To my satisfaction, my words finally seem to shake this chick out of her self-assured, holier-than-thou act.

"No," she admits, looking down. "I don't." She hesitates. "To be honest, that's part of the reason we're keeping her for a few days. Not that she doesn't need care, but... Well, let's just say we're using an abundance of caution."

Aha. So, she *does* think the guy's bad news. *Fuckin' finally.* My blood pressure falls a little bit.

"So, why can't you keep him away from her since he got in a fight with me yesterday?" I challenge. "You can say he's violent, and poses a threat to the other patients?"

"Well..." Her mouth twitches just a little. "As I understand it, technically, *you* were the one who hit *him*. So, *technically*, if anyone should be thrown out of this hospital, it should be you."

I almost get mad again, but then I see the twinkle in her eyes.

"But you're not gonna do that, are you?" I ask.

She snorts softly. "No. I'm not going to do that. Frankly, I..." she looks down again, as though she shouldn't be saying what she's thinking. "Frankly, I can't say it didn't give me some satisfaction to hear about it." She looks back up at me. "That's not very professional, is it?"

"No, but it's human. The guy's a dirtbag." *Thank fuck.* A chink in her armor.

She purses her full, luscious-looking lips. "Look," she mutters, a crease of stress wrinkling her forehead. "I'm not any happier about all of this than you are, Mr..."

"Rourke."

She frowns. "Rourke's your *last* name?"

"No. Rourke's my first name. Rourke Powers."

"Mr. Powers," she corrects herself. "As I said, I'm not any happier about it than you are. But unfortunately, unless Paisley's mother expressly tells us she doesn't want him visiting her daughter, there's nothing that can be done about it."

"Rourke," I repeat. "And like hell there ain't," I growl. "Like hell there ain't."

6
———
LANEY

The next day, I come into work to find a phalanx of bikers stationed outside of Paisley's room.

Katie is standing at the nurses' station as I walk down the hall. As soon as she catches sight of me, she takes a step forward, her eyes wide and brows raised. "I didn't know what to do with them!" she hisses, glancing backward. "I tried to tell one of them they couldn't be loitering around like that, but they said they're all taking turns visiting their friend."

I roll my eyes. "Like hell they are," I snort, unconsciously repeating Rourke's phrase. I wasn't sure to make of his cryptic remark yesterday. But now it's obvious what he meant.

Katie tells me that the bikers have been here for over an hour. As she's talking, an older couple comes down the hall. They pass by the crowd of tattooed men, and skitter toward the far side of the corridor, the woman clutching nervously at the man's arm. Once they're past the group, they avert their eyes and walk as quickly as possible toward the elevators.

"Oh, lord," I mutter. "This isn't going to work."

Taking a deep breath, I square my shoulders and walk toward the men. When I get to the edge of the group, I scan for Rourke, since he's the only one besides the patient called Bear that I've actually spoken to. Not seeing him, though, I clear my throat and speak up.

"Excuse me," I call.

The half-dozen men all turn to look at me. It's a virtual wall of muscle, testosterone and ink. As their eyes settle on me in unison, my stomach does an unpleasant flip. Maybe this wasn't such a good idea after all.

"I'm... uh..." I falter.

I start to lose my nerve, but then think of a way that might buy me some cred and get them to take me seriously.

"I'm looking for Rourke," I announce in a clear, strong voice.

The reaction I get is not what I was hoping for. One by one, they glance at each other, and start snickering. One does a wolf whistle. More than a couple of them look me up and down, so boldly I feel naked.

"You need Rourke, do ya?" one of them chuckles. "I bet he's more than happy to give you what you want. But if he ain't, I'm willing to help you out, darlin'."

My face gets hot when I realize what he's implying. I want to shoot back that is *not* what I meant, but I get the impression that the more I protest, the more they'll razz me.

"Look," I try again, trying desperately to maintain at least a shred of professional demeanor. "I need to talk to him. Can you please tell me if you know where he is?"

More laughter and hoots great my question. Thankfully, one of the men takes pity on me.

"He's in there, darlin'," he smirks, lifting his chin toward Paisley's room.

"Seriously?" Shaking my head in disbelief, I turn toward the half-open door and push inside.

The sight that greets me stops me in my tracks.

Paisley is sitting up in bed, laughing and grinning like crazy. Beside her is a stuffed rabbit almost as big as she is. In the chair facing her, Rourke is doing *coin tricks*. Neither one of them notices me at first, and I stare in fascination as Rourke reaches his arm forward and pulls a quarter from the stuffed rabbit's ear.

"Huh," Rourke says, feigning puzzlement. "I dunno where all this money's coming from, but it sure as heck ain't mine. I guess it belongs to you."

Rourke holds out the quarter, and waits. Paisley shyly dips her head, then reaches her palm outward. Rourke drops the coin, and Paisley's fingers close around it. The tight fist she forms makes one thing clear: this is not a kid who takes money for granted.

I clear my throat, which suddenly feels like it has a lump in it.

"Good morning, Paisley. Do you remember me? Laney, from yesterday?"

She glances over and gives me a shy smile. "Hi!"

"How are you doing today?" I ask, taking a step forward.

"Good! Rourke got me this!" She reaches around the stuffed rabbit with her non-broken arm and squeezes it to her like a long-lost friend.

"Wow, what a nice rabbit!" I enthuse. "Have you named him yet?"

"It's a her," Paisley corrects me. "Her name is Bunnifer."

"That's a great name," I say, stifling a giggle. Turning to Rourke, I say, "Can I please have a quick word with you? Outside?"

Rourke frowns, then shrugs. "Sure." He gets to his feet, and reaches toward Paisley, pulling a quarter out from behind her ear, as well. "You're just full of money today," he tells her, holding it up. He drops it into her hand, where it clinks against the first one.

As Rourke follows me out of the room, I try not to be self-conscious that he might be staring at my butt. Our appearance in the hallway sparks a fresh round of hoots and catcalls, but Rourke tells the men to shut up, and they simmer down after a second.

"Okay, what do you want to talk to me about?" he asks when we've passed them.

"Let's go somewhere a little quieter," I reply, gesturing down the hall. "There's a family lounge past the elevator bays."

As the two of us walk down the hall side by side, I'm once again acutely aware of how large he is. It's amazing that Paisley isn't intimidated by him. On the contrary, she seems to trust him completely. And I have to admit, the more I see him around her, the more I'd be shocked if he hurt her. As scary and rough as he is, he seems completely gentle where she's concerned.

Unlike her mother's boyfriend.

"The family lounge is right in here," I murmur, turning into a small room on the left-hand side of the hall. The room itself is unoccupied save for one person, one of the janitorial staff who must be on break. He's immersed in his phone, but when he looks up and sees me he quickly stands up and exits the room with a look of apology.

"What was that about?" Rourke queries.

"This isn't a break room," I explain. "Hospital staff aren't supposed to be in here unless they're using the room to talk with patients or their families."

The room itself is sparsely furnished and painted in warm tones, with a sink, microwave, a single-serve coffee maker, and stacks of paper beverage cups. I close the door so we won't be disturbed. When I turn back to Rourke, I see his mouth curve into a smirk.

"You don't waste any time," he chuckles. "If you wanted to jump my bones, you could've just asked."

I start to protest, feeling my face begin to flush. But then I see the glint in his eye and realize he's joking. *Probably.*

"Look," I start, pretending to ignore his words. "I know what you're trying to do. But you can't. It's against hospital policy."

"Against hospital policy for my brothers to visit Bear?" he asks innocently.

I sigh. "Don't do that."

"Don't do what?"

"Don't pretend. Not with me." I take a deep breath, hesitating, and then let it out. "I know we're both worried about Paisley. And I get that you're trying to protect her. But the hospital isn't going to let your club stand guard outside her room twenty-four seven."

"Don't need to do it twenty-four seven," he counters. "Just during visiting hours."

"Rourke..."

My voice trails off, because I don't know what to say. His gaze jumps to mine, and I realize I've never actually called him by his first name before. Here in this room, alone just the two us, the word feels intimate, hanging there between us. Almost like I've somehow crossed an invisible line that was keeping us on opposite sides of this problem.

I really should be doing a better job of keeping my professional bearing with him. But every time I try, he cuts right through it. As though he knows it's B.S. Fundamentally, there's something about Rourke that makes me feel utterly without defenses.

My stomach is fluttering nervously. I can't figure out why it is that he has this much of an effect on me. And worse, I can't decide whether I hate it or not.

For a long moment Rourke's eyes linger on my face, dark and penetrating. I realize I haven't said anything since calling him by his name. I try to look away, but it's as though he's pinned me like a butterfly. My heart begins to speed up and thud in my chest.

Finally, I manage to break his gaze.

"You're good with her," I say softly, looking down.

"I had a little sister growing up," he replies, a touch gruffly. "I ain't that great with kids, but I had to babysit her a fair amount. I guess it comes back to you."

Rourke has a little sister. It's a strange concept to wrap my head around. Somehow, he doesn't seem like someone who has a family — or even a childhood. It's almost like he born just like this: Rugged. Hard. All man.

"How long you gonna keep her here?" Rourke asks. His deep baritone is almost like a caress — low and intimate. My body reacts almost viscerally to it. I find myself struggling against a growing attraction to this man that I barely know. I don't know what it is about him that makes me want to push away all the layers of our respective existences that are separating us right now. The very layers that are protecting me from something I should probably be a lot more afraid of than I am.

And that in itself shakes me.

Instinctively, I retreat into the persona I use whenever need to reestablish a professional distance here at work. "That's not information I can give out to someone who's not a member of the family," I begin.

But then, I stop, suddenly hating the officious tone I'm taking with him.

I risk a look at him and see that he's scowling. He sees exactly what I'm doing. Suddenly, I'm a little ashamed of myself. I blow out a breath and try again.

"Look, I'm sorry. But..." I continue, biting my lip. "I'm doing my best to make sure that Paisley is going to be safe when she leaves here. I promise you that."

"You're worried about her, too," he says. Almost imperceptibly, his eyes lose a little of their hardness.

"Yes. I am." I think back to the bruise on Paisley's arm. The one I still haven't managed to talk to Bethany about yet.

"I'm doin' something about it while she's here," Rourke continues. "But what about when she goes home? Her mom's asshole boyfriend will still be there. You can't protect her then." His jaw sets, and he points a thumb to his chest. "But I can."

"Rourke, what are you —" I begin, but a commotion outside stops me.

"Oh, shit," he mutters, and pulls open the door.

7

ROURKE

Sure enough, when we step out into the hallway, Mickey is here, surrounded by the Lords. He's shouting and gesturing, taking feinting half-steps forward, like he's gonna hit Dante.

Even though I'm mad, I bust out laughing at what a dipshit he is. Dante could fuckin' flatten Mickey's dumb ass with one punch.

Laney cuts a sharp look at me, but doesn't ask why I'm laughing. When we get to the crowd, Dipshit sees me and starts yelling, "This is a free country! I got every right to be here."

"Sure as shit is," I agree, coming to a stop in front of him as Dante and Rogue grab him by the shoulders. "Ain't no one stopping you from being in this hospital." I nod at Paisley's room. "Right up to that doorway, there. The second you cross that threshold, you're dead meat, son."

"You ain't got no right!" he yells.

"No? Well, I'm still doin' it." I cross my arms. "You gonna calm the hell down, or do I have to have my brothers take you outside and *convince* you to calm down?"

"What is going on here?"

A male voice I don't recognize booms out in the hall. I turn as a skinny guy with slicked back nineties hair and an expensive suit comes charging toward us.

"Who's this little prick?" mutters Dante.

Beside me, Laney groans. "Blake Barber," she answers, half to herself. "He's the main hospital administrator. Basically, my boss."

"What is going on here?" Blake Fucking Fancy Motherfucker Barber says again as he comes to a stop in front of us. He skims over all of us with his eyes, then addresses Laney like we're not even goddamn here.

"Who are these people, and why are they causing a disruption in my hospital?"

My hospital. Oh, brother.

"This asshole is the one causing the disruption," Rogue growls, shaking Mickey by the shoulder. "We're just makin' sure he *stops* making the disruption."

"Get your fuckin' hands off me!" Mickey yells, starting to struggle. But even though he's ripped from the obvious hours he spends pumping iron at the gym, he ain't got the fighting skills God gave a duck. Rogue grabs his arm and yanks it behind him, bending his elbow up hard. Mickey cries out and stops struggling instantly.

Fuckin' pussy.

"See what I mean?" Rogue grins. "Causin' a disruption."

"The hospital has security on staff," Blake Fucking Barber retorts. "It's their job to take care of disruptions. Not yours." His eyes narrow. "And right now, you people are doing your share of disrupting yourself."

I swear to Christ, if he says that fuckin' word again, I'm gonna shove my fist straight down his throat.

Laney swallows and speaks up. "Blake," she says in a soothing voice. "These men have every right to be here. They're visiting their friend, in that room there. They've been nothing but respectful of the rules. If there's a problem here, I'm sure they didn't start it."

Huh. A day ago, I'm pretty sure Laney would have sided with the administrator asshole. She probably would have been glad to see all of us thrown out on our ears.

Looks like she's figured out we aren't the enemies here. Maybe she's not as stuck up as I thought she was.

The administrator guy's eyes slide down to Laney's tits. She notices it, too.

By the way she purses her lips in response, it's pretty clear she doesn't like it one bit.

And by the lack of surprise on her face, it's also pretty clear it ain't the first time.

Finally, his eyes go back up to her face. He sucks on his teeth for a second, like he's evaluating something. Laney's eyes flicker, but she doesn't look away.

"You all need to break this up," he announces, looking at my brothers. "I cannot have gang fights going on in my hospital." He turns to me then, somehow deciding I'm the leader. "You will not loiter in the hall. Here or anywhere else. Am I understood?"

I will hand it to this self-important prick. He actually seems to think my brothers and I are gonna listen to him. He seems to thinks we give a fuck what he thinks.

"Stop us," I say.

My calm tone takes him by surprise. Flinching a little, he takes a step back. Just then, Paisley's mom comes running down the hall towards us.

"What's going on?" she stammers, looking at Mickey.

"Your boyfriend's gettin' taught some manners," I tell her.

"Mickey..." she murmurs plaintively, her face crumpling. "Please don't..."

Angrily, he wrestles himself away from Rogue and Dante. "I ain't done a damn thing!" he explodes. Grabbing her arm, he yanks her toward him, pulling her with him toward the elevators.

Laney takes a half-step forward, like she wants to help the

mom. The look on her face as she watches them go is full of shock and sadness.

Mickey turns back to us as he struts down the hall, flipping the bird as he tries to salvage what's left of his dignity. "I ain't gonna put up with this shit!" I hear him shouting as they go.

I consider going after him. But as I glance over at Laney's crumpled expression, I decide against it.

With Mickey gone, the tension in the hallways eases. But the administrator prick isn't done with his pissing contest.

"I don't want to hear about any more trouble from you. Understood?" he announces. He raises a hand and starts to point a finger at me, but I think the look I give him convinces him pretty quick it ain't a good idea.

He lowers his hand.

"Look," I growl at Blake Fucking Pissant Barber. "You get that ass wipe outta here," I say, flicking my thumb toward Mickey's retreating form, "And you won't have anything to worry about. He's the only one we got a problem with around here." *Other than you, that is.*

Instead of replying to me, he turns to Laney. "I need to see you in my office," he tells her in a clipped voice. "Now."

Laney shoots me a look, rolling her eyes. *Keep things calm*, she mouths at me as she turns away.

As I watch them go, Yoda comes up beside me.

"So, that asshole was Mickey, eh?" he asks.

"Yeah."

"Piece of shit."

"Yeah."

"I got the intel you asked for."

"Oh yeah?" I turn to him. "Good deal. You find out anything interesting?"

He nods. "Full name's Michael King. No job that I can tell. Looks like Paisley's mom supports him. She's an exotic dancer at that strip joint over in Kendrick."

My ears perk up. "The one owned by Jimmy Mazur?"

"Yup."

Huh. Interesting. Mazur runs a protection racket and loan shark biz. His one legitimate business, the strip club, is a front for a small-time prostitution operation. Not to mention an illegal gambling casino in the back of the place.

If Paisley's mom works there, she's either just stripping or hooking, too. Either way, it's gotta be because she's desperate for money, or she's hooked on drugs.

From the looks of her, she's not strung out. I'd say it's probably the former. Which makes sense if she's supporting Mickey.

"Mickey got any association with Jimmy Mazur?" I ask.

"Oh yeah." Yoda snorts. "Apparently our buddy Mickey's got a gambling problem. I guess he met Paisley's ma at the club. I hear he's also got a nose for the snow, when he can get it. And rock when he can't."

"Fuck." It does not make me happy to hear that the man who spends time around Paisley has a drug habit.

"Yeah," Yoda says drily. "My source over at Mazur's said Mickey did a good job of charming Paisley's mom at first. Talked a big game about how he was gonna make it big off bein' a professional poker player." He eyes me. "They're living at the Sunrise Motel right now. Got kicked out of the place they were living in a couple weeks ago."

"Why'd they get kicked out?"

"According to my source at Mazur's place, Paisley's ma told her Mickey got drunk and disorderly one too many times."

"That ain't hard to believe," I remark. "You talk to Mazur yourself while you where there?"

"Nah. Just to Amber, one of the dancers there," Yoda shrugs.

"Huh." I pause for a couple of seconds, lost in thought. "Yoda," I finally say, "why don't you and me take a ride back down to Mazur's place tomorrow?" I suggest. "I got some questions I wanna ask Jimmy myself."

"Fine by me," he says with a leering grin. "The scenery's always good, at least."

I laugh and tell him to get hold of Mazur on the phone in the meantime, to make sure he's gonna be around when we stop by.

I decide I need to start keeping closer tabs on Mickey King. Who he hangs around with. Who might be out to get him for an unpaid debt.

And most of all, how likely it is Paisley and her mom might end up caught in the middle of it all.

8

LANEY

I know I'm in for a dressing down from Blake Barber even before we get to his office. All the way there, I'm arguing with him in my mind, preparing my defense. Explaining how I had no control over the crowd of bikers in the hallway outside Paisley's room.

So I'm taken a little by surprise when, once his office door closes behind me, Blake turns around with an indulgent smile on his face.

"Laney, Laney," he begins, leaning back against his desk and crossing his arms. "You need to learn how to let me, help you."

"I'm sorry?" I stammer.

With a soft chuckle, he continues. "I understand that you lost control of the situation down there. That in itself isn't a crime. But where you went wrong is not calling security, or me."

I stare at him. With his expensive, well-tailored suit, he looks every inch the hospital executive. I know from what he's told me — repeatedly — that he has a master's degree in health care administration from the University of Denver. What he's doing as an administrator in a small-town hospital like this, I don't know.

But he acts for all the world like he's some hyper-important busi-
nessman. Like Christian Grey or something. Without the
playroom.

At least, I hope so. *Gross.*

I tamp down my impulse to tell him I did not lose control of
one damn thing. Being confrontational with my boss isn't likely
to do me much good here.

"Blake," I say instead, keeping my tone reasonable. "As I said
before, those bikers did nothing wrong. They were merely
visiting their friend. The only problem we had down there was
the boyfriend of that mom of the patient across the hall. He
created the *disruption*, not them."

I consciously use his word, working hard to keep any hint of
mockery out of my voice.

"I reserve the right to make my own judgment about what I
saw," Blake responds with a tinge of irritation. "The point is, in
the future, I expect you to do a better job of being proactive."

Blake moves behind his desk and sits down, motioning for me
to take the chair across from him. He leans forward, elbows on
his desk, his long, thin fingers laced in front of him. His nails are
cut perfectly straight across, professionally manicured and buffed
to a polish. Distracted, I notice how pale and soft-looking the skin
of his hands is. How different they are from Rourke's — strong,
rough, and square. The two men couldn't be more different,
really. Blake's power comes from his title, and his position behind
this desk in an office with his name on the door. Rourke's
strength comes from himself. From some inner force inside him.
He doesn't need fancy clothes or titles to hide behind.

Blake clears his throat. I look up guiltily, realizing I was practically daydreaming. When my eyes find his face, I suppress a
moue of disgust.

"Now." Blake hunches forward a little more, giving me a direct
look. "Enough about those bikers." His lip curls at the word. "I
need to know what the situation is with the patient and her

mother. Is there any reason to believe your professional involvement is needed here?"

I need to tread lightly here. Blake has been known to override my decisions in the past. And as the hospital's CEO, he's brought a single-minded focus on Morningside's financial bottom line that means he'll choose saving a little money over patient care every time. "The little girl — Paisley — came in with a broken arm and head trauma. I was brought in just to make sure there was no evidence of abuse."

He purses his lips. "How much longer until the girl is released?"

"I'm not sure," I hesitate. "I know the admitting doctor wanted to run some tests on her. To make sure the symptoms of concussion aren't an indication of something more serious."

"Does the mother have insurance?" Blake asks pointedly.

"I..." My brain races for an answer that will satisfy him, but I know there isn't one. The truth is, Bethany is uninsured, and I'm sure he suspects this.

"We are not a charity organization," he snaps. "And the girl is not in any immediate danger, is she?"

"No, but—"

"Who's the attending doctor on staff?" he asks. "No, don't bother answering that. I'll find out myself." Blake pushes himself up to a stand and turns away. "I think it's time for her to be discharged."

"Blake, please..." I begin. Belatedly, I curse myself for not trying the catch-more-flies-with-honey approach with him from the outset. I know from experience how much he loves being flattered — loves having his ego stroked. But I've been careful not to do anything that could be construed as leading him on, afraid of what the consequences might be. Because Blake has been trying to get me to go out with him — or at least to sleep with him — since before I was even hired here.

I didn't realize how bad it would be at first. Oh, sure, he was a little creepy during the interview. But call me naive, I brushed it off. And I really wanted this job, so I told myself I was probably imagining things.

Turns out, I definitely was not.

The memory of the first few months of my employment here at Morningside Hospital makes a cold lump of ice form in my stomach. Blake has never quite forgiven me for turning him down when he asked me out on a date a few days after I was hired at Morningside. Ever since then, it's been a delicate dance to keep pretending I don't notice or understand the obvious signals he's been sending me. To pretend I don't notice when he brushes up against me in close quarters. To act like I think it's funny when he makes jokes that are really just thinly-veiled sexual innuendoes.

I've worked hard to prove myself at this job. But the longer I'm here, the more I realize that doesn't matter. Because Blake Barber didn't hire me for my qualifications.

The fact is, even though I'm damn good at what I do, that's not why Blake hired me. He hired me because he thought I would put out.

I love my job. I do. But the longer I'm at Morningside, the more I have the sense that I'm on probation with him, and that I'm not measuring up to his expectations. I've been as businesslike as possible, hoping to win him over with my professionalism and work ethic. Beyond that, I try to avoid him as much as possible, figuring the less I'm on his radar, the better. Because my job, no matter how well I do it, depends on Blake's good opinion of me.

The longer I'm here, the more convinced I am that his opinion of me will never be good, because I'll never give him the one thing he wants. As much as I try not to think about it, the reality is clear.

Professionally, I'm on borrowed time.

But right now, none of that really matters. Right now, the most important thing is that I do my best by Paisley. I *need* to talk to her mom about Mickey. I need to find out whether he's a danger to either one of them. To try to help them.

But in order to do that, I need for Paisley to still be in the hospital, where she's safe. I need to buy myself some time. Even if it's only another day.

So, knowing I'll probably pay for it later, I take a step forward and lean over his desk.

"Blake," I breathe, letting my voice go husky. I lower my eyes submissively — despising myself for stooping this low — and make sure I'm bent over just enough that he can see the swell of my breasts through the opening of my blouse. "Could we give it just a *little* longer? I'm really worried about Paisley. And I know Doctor Methaney said he felt she needs more time under observation. Just to make sure."

You would think that a stunt so blatant would never work.

That Blake would see right through what I'm trying to do.

But instead, he takes a good, long look at my boobs, while I pretend not to notice.

Then, with a sigh, he gives me a teasing *what-am-I-going-to-do-with-you* shake of his head.

"All right" he tells me, with a smirk that stops just short of a leer. "I'll let it go for now. But Laney, I expect you to check in with me daily and let me know what her progress is. I need reports on when the doctors plan to discharge her."

"Understood."

"And make sure those bikers stop congregating in the hallway," he says, his lip curling in distaste. "I'm relying on you to call security if they won't comply."

I want to argue with him. But at this point, I figure I should quit while I'm ahead.

So instead, I assure him I will.

"Thank you, Blake," I say breathily.

Then I duck out of there before he can say anything else.

I just bought myself a few more days. I'd better make it count.

I guess it doesn't matter that I hate myself for the way I did it.

And more than anything, I hope what I did back there won't come back to bite me in the ass.

9

ROURKE

Yoda comes with me on a ride down to Mazur's place, the Lucky Strike. It's early in the day, so there's hardly anyone in the place when we get there, but there's no windows, so once you're inside it could be midnight or noon and you'd never know it.

I've been to the Strike a few times. It's not really my scene — too depressing — but it serves a purpose, I guess. The interior's like the inside of a fuckin' vagina, all done up in pinks and satin. The place smells like booze and cigarettes. Usually, there's music booming, and women workin' the stage, but right now the sound system is on low, and it looks like the performers are taking a break.

Yoda and I belly up to the bar in the back. I signal to the bartender for a shot, and Yoda gets the same. A couple of girls come over, squeezed into tiny little outfits that put their tits and ass on full display. A chestnut-haired beauty immediately slides halfway onto Yoda's lap — as far as she can as he sits on the bar stool, anyway.

"You came back for me!" she coos, nuzzling his ear. "I missed you."

ins at me. "This is Amber."

_aisy," the blond with her announces. She's less stacked than Amber, but her face is prettier. She sidles up to me, wraps one arm around my neck, and looks up at me with her painted doe eyes. "I've been waiting for you all day."

I can't say I'm not tempted. More out of habit than anything, I realize. Daisy ain't got nothin' on display I haven't seen before. I could take her into a back room and spend a little time with her, but it doesn't really sound all that appealing, in the end. It'd be more like takin' a handful of chips because the bag's sitting there in front of you, not because you're hungry.

"I hate to tell you darlin'," but you're gonna have to wait a little longer," I tell her, peeling her arm off me. "I need to talk to your boss. He around?"

Daisy gives me a pout and looks like she wants to argue with me, but she must see in my eyes that I'm not buyin' what she's sellin'. Shooting her friend a look, she disappears into the back, swishing her tail feathers as she goes.

A minute later, Jimmy Mazur comes out, flanked by a big, lunking monstrosity of a man standing almost seven feet tall. Mazur introduces him as Dewey. There's no mistaking him as anything other than Mazur's bodyguard. Mazur himself is almost as wide as he is tall. He's like a goddamn Polish meatball: beefy, completely round, and smelling like onions.

"What can I do for you gentlemen?" he booms, raising his arms wide. He gives us a yellow-toothed grin, and claps Yoda on the back. "The girls tol' me you stopped by yesterday, too."

"Yeah. I came by to get a lap dance and some intel." Yoda lifts his chin toward me. "Rourke wanted to come back and follow up on some shit."

Jimmy eyes our empty shot glasses. "You want another drink? On the house! Then we go sit over there and talk," he announces, pointing to a low, round table off to one side of the stage.

Yoda and I let the bartender grab us a couple of beers, and we go sit down with Mazur. Dewey lurches behind us, standing like Frankenstein's fuckin' monster off to one side.

"Does he talk?" I ask, jerking my thumb toward him.

"He talks when I want him to." Jimmy raises his voice. "Say somethin', Dewey."

"Hello," glowers Dewey.

"So, whaddya wanna talk to me about?" Mazur asks. "Yoda said somethin' about Mickey King?"

"Yeah. What's the story with him? You've known him a while?"

"Yeah. He comes around here a lot. His girl, Bethany works here as a dancer."

"How long as she worked here?"

"About... six months, maybe?" Mazur shrugs. "More or less. Mickey's been comin' here a lot longer than that, though."

"He come here for the girls?" I press. "Or to gamble?"

"Both, I guess. But more for the gamblin'. And he don't really go with the girls anymore." Mazur lowers his voice. "Except when Bethany ain't around, that is."

Yoda's nostrils flare. "He any good at gambling?"

Mazur barks out a laugh. "Mickey? Nah. He sucks at it. He wins just enough to keep him comin' back. His M.O. is, he comes in with a wad of money, loses it, goes in the hole, borrows more money from me, and loses that. Then he disappears for a few days, or a few weeks, 'til he can scrape up the money and pay me back. Then the cycle starts all over again." His expression turns sour. "Only lately he ain't been payin' me back."

"What do you mean?" I ask.

Mazur exhales in disgust, wafting onion breath across the table. "Fuckin' Mickey. He's been gambling back there, losin' his shirt to the Vietnamese. I bailed his stupid ass out more times... The asshole used to pay me back. Now lately, I ain't hardly seen him. Because he owes me, you know? He keeps tellin' me Bethany will pay me."

"How's she gonna do that?" Yoda asks. "She ain't got a pot to piss in, from what I understand."

Mazur shoots him a leer. "Bethany's a dancer here. But she could do a lot more, if you know what I mean. Lotsa guys here would pay good money to get with that. She could pay off his debts pretty fast, if she wanted to work overtime."

Next to me, Yoda tenses, to my surprise. "That's a hell of a fucked up thing, Mazur, expectin' her to pay for his debt like that," he spits out.

Mazur shrugs and shows his palms. "Hey, I ain't forcin' anyone. She don't wanna do it, she doesn't do it."

"Does Mickey have any other sources of income that you know of?" I ask.

Mazur scoffs. "He's mostly a petty thug. Always running some low-level scam or another. You know the type. Stealin' stuff off the backs of trucks and selling it, shit like that. Never hangs onto it for long. Mickey is the kind of guy who'd be easy to talk into any dumbass scheme to make some fast cash. That dumb shit always thinks he's one step away from the big break that's gonna make him a millionaire."

"That sounds about right," I say filing that away for later. "You got anything else you can tell us?"

"I dunno." Mazur peers at me over his round, gin-blossomed cheeks. "What do you want with him, anyway?"

"Nothing in particular. He's been spending some time in our territory. I'm just tryin' to figure out how much of an inconvenience he's gonna be."

"For the Lords?" Mazur laughs. "He's just a big loud mouth, with nothin' behind it. Too smart to realize he's dumb."

"He got any debts that you know?" I press. "Other than you?"

"Yeah, probably." Mazur looks down at the table for a moment, frowning. "You know what I think? I think he's mixed up with the Vietnamese guys he gambles with sometimes in the back of my club."

"You mean you think he owes them money, too?"

"Yeah. Or at least, he's in business with them and he's gonna fuck it up. I hear them talkin' sometimes when they're playin' cards back there. About jobs he's doin' for them. It wouldn't be the first time, either." Mazur chuckles to himself. "You've seen Mickey, right? I mean up close? You know that missing finger on his right hand?"

"Yeah."

"He got it cut off by some Asian wannabe gangster up in Cincy. This crew that thinks they're part of Yakuza or something. Word is, they cut his pinky off to settle a debt." He shakes his head. "And I bet you anything, that dumb shit's gonna go right back for more."

We thank Mazur for his time, and leave the club. To my surprise, the usually unexcitable Yoda is scowling and angry.

"Bethany don't belong with that weak-ass pussy," he mutters. "That fuckin' Mickey's no better than a goddamn pimp."

I look over at him, raising a brow, but I don't say anything. He's right, of course. Hey, I got no issue with a woman doin' whatever she wants with her body. But it takes a special brand of shitbucket to wanna pimp out your girlfriend.

As we head back to Ironwood on our bikes, I think about everything we just learned from Mazur. I'm starting to get a fuller picture of Mickey King. What I see is a small-time thug, playing at being a big shot. A guy who's down on his luck. A guy who needs a woman he can boss around, and her job to keep a roof over his head.

A guy with small prospects and a big ego.

A guy who isn't all that bright. Or with all that much to lose.

10

LANEY

The next morning, as soon as I get to work, I make it a point to go up to the second floor to finally have the conversation I'm dreading with Paisley's mother.

When I get upstairs, I'm immediately relieved to see there's only one biker stationed outside her room. At least for the moment, he's probably not enough to draw Blake's attention. I mentally shift that problem to second place.

Bethany is already there in the room with Paisley. The shades are partially drawn against the bright morning sun, which I'm assuming is because of Paisley's light sensitivity due to the concussion. Mickey, thankfully, is nowhere to be seen.

I make small talk with the two of them for a few minutes. Paisley's not quite as subdued as she was last time I saw her. Her little face is still banged up, and she still seems tired, but I note that her coloring looks better. I ask her a few questions about school, and what her favorite games and shows are. In spite of still not feeling great, she's alert, and seems comfortable around her mother, and not agitated or afraid. Good signs all.

When I turn Bethany and ask if I can speak to her outside for a few minutes, she gives me a worried frown.

"Is this about Mickey?" she asks.

Paisley immediately looks up, her eyes darting from her mother to me.

"Partly," I nod, giving them both what I hope is a reassuring smile. "Come on. Let's go talk in the family lounge. Paisley, I'm gonna go talk to your mom for a few minutes, okay? We'll be right back."

I take Bethany into the small beige room where I talked to Rourke earlier. Closing the door, I motion for her to sit down on the couch, then take the chair next to her.

"She's looking better today," I begin. "That must be a relief."

"It is," she agrees. She looks down at her hands. Taking a shaky breath, she continues. "I know I should never have left her alone at that age. It's just that I have to work. And just now, I can't afford a babysitter all the time. She's supposed to stay in the room with the door locked whenever I'm gone. She knows better than to leave."

"And," I continue, hesitating. "What about Mickey? Does he ever take care of her when you're at work?"

"Oh, Mickey..." Bethany laughs nervously. "He's not all that crazy about kids. I don't ask him to do that stuff."

Her body immediately tenses up at the mention of her boyfriend. If I keep going with this line of conversation, I'm pretty sure she'll shut down. So I back off a bit and switch gears.

"Has the doctor been by recently to talk to you about Paisley's condition?" I ask delicately.

"Yeah." Bethany clasps her hands together. "He said her concussion doesn't seem to have caused any internal bleeding or anything like that. Paisley's still feeling sick to her stomach, and she still has a headache, but the doctor thinks both of those things will go away with time. I just have to keep her quiet and make sure she sleeps enough. Limit screen time. And he said she might have trouble concentrating on schoolwork and stuff for a while."

"That's good to hear." I nod. "Will you have trouble keeping an eye on her, after she's discharged? I'm guessing it will be hard for you to take off from your job."

"I'll make it work," Bethany retorts, an edge in her voice. "Somehow." She shifts her body toward me and looks me in the eyes. "I love my little girl," she says fiercely. "I'm not a bad mother."

"Bethany." I let out a sigh. "I know you do. I know things are hard right now. Please believe me, that I'm trying to help you. I know this is a scary time. And I'm sure that money worries are only making it scarier." I wait a beat, then continue, more gently.

"One of my jobs here at the hospital is to locate resources, to help patients and their families with after-hospital care," I say. "And to the extent possible, with help with figuring out how to manage the burden of your hospital bills. I can start working on that for you now, if you'd like. Maybe we can have some sort of a plan in place by the time Paisley gets the okay to be discharged."

"Really?" Bethany's eyes grow wide with disbelief.

I nod. "Really. I can't work magic. But I'll do what I can."

The smile she gives me is so tremulous, so full of hope, that it makes my stomach hurt. I can't imagine how hard it must be for her, to feel so alone in the world, raising a child by herself without any kind of help. Spontaneously, I reach out and put my hand over hers.

"We'll figure it out," I tell her.

"Thank you," she whispers.

"Don't thank me until I've actually delivered," I joke, to lighten the mood a little. My voice wobbles, but she doesn't seem to notice. She ducks her head, swiping at her eyes.

"Bethany," I say, more softly now. "There's something else I need to talk to you about. Okay?"

"This is the Mickey part, right?" Bethany laughs shakily. "I know he's been causing problems. He gets riled easy. He doesn't do very well with authority."

"It's not about the altercations in the hallway," I tell her. "Although they definitely are not helpful."

"What is it then?" she asks, clearly apprehensive.

I take a deep breath.

"When Paisley was admitted, the doctor noticed a bruise on her upper arm that seemed consistent with a hand grabbing her." I wait a beat. "A large hand."

"Please..." Bethany moans. "Please, it's not what you think..."

"I don't think anything. Yet," I say carefully. "Which is why I'm asking you to tell me what *you* think?"

She swallows, her eyes darting around the room before coming to rest on me. She looks stricken.

"That happened the night before the accident," she half-whispers. "We fought about it, and I put him out of the house — out of the motel room where we're staying, I mean. He was gone all night. He must have come back the next afternoon, though. Paisley told me he was there when she got home from school."

"I see."

Bethany pleads with me now. "I swear, he's never done anything like that before. Mickey doesn't really like kids, like I said. And I know sometimes Paisley gets on his nerves. But he's never hurt her before that. I swear to God he hasn't!"

Her voice rises as she talks. I look down at her hands, which are clenched tightly together. The skin of her fingers is white.

"Please," she repeats, her voice dropping to a whisper. "I would never let him hurt my baby. Please believe me!"

I swallow. "I know you wouldn't. But the fact is, he *did*." I pause. "And in my experience, it's not likely to be the last time."

She looks away.

"Bethany," I murmur. "Under the circumstances, do you think that maybe the bikers outside Paisley's door have it right? That maybe it might be better to tell the hospital Mickey shouldn't have visitor's rights to her?"

She looks back at me and shakes her head. "If he can't come in here, he's not gonna let me come either."

As kindly as I can, I say, "You know you don't need his permission, right?"

"I know... It's just... he gets mad, and when he gets like that it isn't worth going against him." Bethany's voice cracks. "I'm sure you think I'm being stupid and weak. I know he's... that he's not the best guy. But sometimes it's so hard to be alone, you know?" She takes another rough swipe at her eyes. "I don't have money. I don't have a college degree, like you do. I just... Sometimes you just don't have the strength to do it all alone. But you've stopped believing someone good will ever come along. So you settle for good *enough*."

Her words bring me up short.

"I know," I say, nodding quietly. "I'm sure you don't believe me. But I understand."

I'm sure she thinks I'm judging her right now. That I couldn't possibly know what it's like to be her.

And she's right, I don't. Not exactly.

But I've seen the way my mom has always danced around my father's moods. How much she's put up with, for the status of being a prominent politician's wife. How much she's erased herself.

As I sit and look at Bethany, I think of the last time I saw my mother in person. It was last Christmas. Against my better judgment, I went home for their annual big deal holiday party. As usual, it was a grandiose affair, with all the prominent bigwigs of Louisville in attendance. It's the kind of event that gets written up in the society pages of the paper.

The house looked beautiful, as always, professionally decorated inside and out. My father, handsome as ever, was king of his domain, greeting and glad-handing the guests all night long. My mother looked beautiful as well, with her always-perfect silver bob, flawless makeup, and a sequined dress that cost more than my monthly rent. And as always, she sparkled as Senator Hart's wife, smiling and laughing as she held her champagne flute and stood by my his side, beaming up at him as he proposed a toast to old friends and new.

But my strongest memory of that night isn't the party itself. It's how all evening long, I knew my mother's makeup — so carefully applied by her in the privacy of her dressing room — was extra thick to hide the bruise that was forming along her jaw.

The bruise given to her by my father that afternoon, when she told him there had been a mixup with the caterers and they wouldn't be arriving until fifteen minutes after the party was scheduled to begin.

I've seen how much my mother has sacrificed of herself. How hard she's worked to settle for what she thinks is *good enough*.

And I'm afraid I'm about to watch my sister do the same thing when she marries Nick Harris.

Unlike Bethany, at least my mother and sister have the advantage of financial security. They have a life that looks to the outside world like the ultimate dream of happiness and success. I guess that's enough for them to convince themselves it's all worth it.

But *is* it enough? Is it really worth it?

From the outside, most people would say my mother and sister have it made.

From the outside, most people wouldn't see any similarities at all between them and the desperate, lonely woman sitting across from me right now.

But I sure do.

And what I see in front of me is a woman who needs help. And a woman whose daughter will learn her lessons about relationships from watching her mother. Just like I learned from watching my parents.

Suddenly, I want to do everything I can to make sure that the lessons Paisley learns are the right ones.

"I'll do everything I can to help you, Bethany," I say fiercely. "I promise. In the meantime, you just focus on doing what's best for Paisley."

11

ROURKE

Bear gets out of the hospital two days later. From the looks on the faces of the hospital staff when I get there to help spring him out, there's going to be one hell of a celebration once he's gone.

The nurses don't look as scared now when they pass one of the Lords as they did the first day. Instead, they look irritated. Like seeing one of us reminds them of the surly motherfucker in room two-seventeen.

Bear refused Axel's offer to bring him back to the clubhouse from the hospital. A couple of the brothers are taking him to his house instead. Since he's still recovering from the stab wound, one of the prospects is gonna be his errand boy for a few days, until he gets back on his feet.

I can't help but shake my head at the thought of it. That prospect is gonna hate his life for a while, that's for certain.

Axel and I are standing out in the hallway the morning Bear gets discharged. We're leaning against a wall, watching the three ring circus of nurses trying to get Bear to ride out of this place in a wheelchair. I'm getting a pretty good laugh out of the whole damn thing. Even Axel, who's usually pretty stone-faced and stoic, is cracking a smile.

"You good with keeping a few brothers here at the hospital during visiting hours for a few days, prez?" I ask as we observe the scene in front of us. "I wanna keep an eye on Paisley's room."

"Yeah, I'm fine with it."

Axel knows the story by now. Paisley's become kind of an unofficial mascot of the club. That kid's gotten more stuffed animals, toys, and candy in the last few days than she probably got for her last damn birthday. And she sure ain't hurting for visitors, either, even when her mom's not here.

"Hospital staff still givin' you grief about the Lords standing guard for her?" Axel asks.

"Don't matter. I think they're gettin' used to it. They don't like the mom's boyfriend, either. When the MC's around, at least he knows he's on notice. Saves them the trouble of keepin' an eye on him themselves." I pause. "I don't think they're gonna keep her here much longer, though. Paisley's doin' good, healing up okay. And from what I can gather, her mom doesn't have insurance."

"You can't protect that kid forever, Rourke." Axel eyes me with a frown.

"The hell I can't."

"What're you gonna do?"

"I dunno yet, exactly."

I'm not gonna lie, I've considered takin' Mickey outside and beating the motherfucker within an inch of his life. Not sure why I haven't yet, to be honest.

Axel doesn't reply. After a couple seconds, he says, "Hey, I need you to go on a run with me. Down to talk to Chaco."

"Down to Louisville?" I frown. "What's up?"

"Dos Santos got fucked, is what. A bunch of his guys got busted at a roadhouse just outside their territory. The cops arrested them all for drunk and disorderly. Trumped up charges, but Chaco thinks it's sending a signal. The Dos Santos cartel is being targeted, and the cops are in on it."

"Turf war," I groan.

"And our shipments are right in the middle of it."

"Fuck me. This is bad."

"Damn right it is," Axel says grimly. "Chaco wants to renegotiate terms. Wants to do it in person. I'm guessing he's gonna tell us he can't get as much product for us as we agreed on. But that ain't gonna fly with the Tanner Springs charter. Angel's got some thirsty buyers who ain't gonna be happy with the club if the supply starts to dry up."

I nod, thinking about the president of the Tanner Springs Lords of Carnage. Angel's an ambitious motherfucker. He's working on building our club into one of the major players in the region.

"Angel know about this yet?"

Axel shakes his head. "I'm gonna wait until I know what the score is before I call him. But I need my VP there with me to be eyes and ears with Chaco. You in?"

"'Course. You takin' anyone else?"

"Yeah. Mal and Dante," he grunts. "Any more than that attracts too much attention on the road."

"When we goin'?"

"Few days. I'll let you know."

"Got ya."

Axel pushes off from the wall and disappears down the hallway.

By now, the nurses have given up on Bear's ever planting his ass in that wheelchair. The short one, Katie, throws up her hands in defeat and storms off, wheeling the chair in front of her. Bear grins — the first time I've seen him crack a smile since he got into this place.

"Jesus Christ, you're an asshole," I call out at him.

"Ah, fuck you," he fires back over his shoulder. "You wouldn't ride in one of those things, either."

"True that," I admit with a laugh.

Bear lifts his chin at me, and then at Rogue, who's standing guard outside Paisley's room. Then, flanked by two other brothers and a prospect, he saunters down the hallway toward freedom, on his own two feet — but not before flipping the bird one final time at room two-seventeen.

Now that the show is over, I turn my attention to the other reason I'm here.

"Hey," I ask a pretty blonde nurse who's just coming out of a room a couple of doors down from Paisley's. "Where can I find that social worker? Laney? She have an office or something?"

The blonde opens her eyes a little wider at me, but otherwise doesn't react. "Her office is on the first floor. In the east wing. There's a directory next to the elevators downstairs that will tell you her office number."

When I get down to the first floor, I find the directory, right where the blonde nurse said it would be. For a second, I don't see Laney's name, but then I realize it's because she's listed under Delaney. I note her last name, too: Hart.

Filing that information away, I head down the hall toward where her office should be.

The door to Laney's office is cracked open about six inches. I rap on it with a knuckle and push it a little wider. She's sitting in front of a laptop, typing, her lower lip caught between her teeth as she concentrates. After a second she looks up. Her eyes flicker in recognition when she sees me.

"Hello," she murmurs, one brow arching.

She's wearing her hair up today, in a bun high on her head that somehow manages to look professional and fuck hot at the same time. A black silk shirt with a low neckline slides softy against her skin, showing off the swell of those breasts I've been dying to touch. The plump lower lip she was biting glistens slightly, pulling at my attention and making my jeans uncomfortably tight as I imagine her wrapping it and its partner around my cock.

"Hey," I mutter. My voice comes out husky. "Can I talk to you for a few?"

Laney shifts her body toward me. "What's up?"

"It's about Paisley."

Laney blinks, then rises in her chair and picks up a small key ring sitting on the desk next to her laptop. "I wouldn't mind grabbing a cup of coffee," she says. "There's a shop on this floor."

"I'll buy you a cup. Come on."

I push the door open the rest of the way and hold it open for her. As she steps through, she raises here eyebrow again. "How gentlemanly of you," she teases.

"That's me. All gentleman."

That, and it gives me the chance to cop a look at that fucking fantastic ass of hers.

She's wearing one of those pencil skirts today, the kind that hugs her thighs. It's the color of ripe plums. The heels she's got on are giving me all sorts of fantasies about takin' her back inside that office, locking the door, and having her strip down until those shoes are the only thing she's got on while I fuck her on the desk.

My cock throbs. I force myself to think of dead puppies and come up beside her.

When we get to the coffee shop, I ask her what she wants to drink, then tell her to go get us a place to sit. I grab our orders, and find her at a small table against the far wall. There's only two other customers, both of them alone, at tables on the other side of the shop.

"Here you go," I say. I set her cup down and grab the chair across from her.

"Thanks." Laney picks up the coffee and takes a quick sip, grimacing slightly. "Hot."

"Yeah. Coffee usually is," I smirk.

"Really?" she asks, narrowing her eyes. "You're going to do this?"

"Do what?"

"Be a jerk." She wrinkles her nose. "You asked me to come talk to you. I'm talking to you."

"Okay, okay. Sorry." I hold up my hands.

"So," she prompts, suddenly all business. "Paisley."

"Yeah." I lean back and look at her. "How much longer is she gonna be in here?"

"In the hospital?" Laney bites her plump lower lip again and stares down at her cup. It's not something she's doing to be sexy — in fact, I doubt she even realizes she's doing it at all — but somehow the gesture always goes straight to my dick.

"Not much longer, unfortunately," she finally says. "I mean, it's good that she's doing better. But..."

"But once she's out of the hospital, she's back with Mickey again," I finish for her.

Laney blows out a breath. "Exactly."

"Yeah. So, I've been thinkin' about that."

"What about?"

"Some way to get Mickey out of the picture."

Laney's eyes widen. "Permanently?"

I have to laugh at her shock. "I don't mean kill him. Jesus."

Though it has crossed my mind.

Not that you need to know that.

Laney looks down, embarrassed, but when she looks back up at me, I can tell she still doesn't get what I'm driving at.

"Look, I'm talking about getting him away from Paisley," I explain. "I dunno. Buy some time. Because it doesn't look to me like Bethany is gonna dump him anytime soon."

"You may be right about that," Laney concedes. "Not as hard

as he'll need to be dumped, anyway. She told me she did kick him out the night before Paisley's accident. But he came back. And she doesn't seem to have the strength right now to get rid of him for good." She sighs. "I suggested she could put him on a list of people who weren't allowed to see Paisley here at the hospital, but she didn't want to do that, either."

"The ass wipe has been comin' around the hospital a bunch of times every day, according to the Lords outside Paisley's room," I tell her. "I can't figure out why, though, since he doesn't seem to even like the kid."

"Control," Laney answers immediately. "It bugs him that he's not calling the shots. And he's really upset about the money he thinks it's costing to keep Paisley here. My guess is he sees Bethany's money as rightfully his. And the more time Paisley's in the hospital, the less of it she has to give him."

"Makes sense," I nod.

I tell her everything I found out about Mickey from Yoda's sniffing around. "Sounds to me like Bethany might be the only thing keepin' him from sleeping out on a park bench somewhere. Seems like most of Mickey's money goes straight to his gambling habit, from what Yoda can tell."

"Crap," she mutters. "He's not going to let Bethany go without a fight. She's his gravy train."

"Can't you file some kind of social work order, or something?" I ask, frustrated. "To keep him away from Paisley?"

Laney sucks in a breath. "It's complicated," she says, peering into her cup. "The short answer is, there's not really enough evidence to do that. The long answer is, anything I do to try to keep Mickey away from Paisley, will end up hurting Bethany and Paisley. And the only evidence I have that Mickey's hurting…"

Laney stops abruptly, her mouth snapping shut. She sneaks a quick glance at me, then looks back down into her cup.

Goddamnit, there's something she's not saying.

"What? Laney, finish your damn sentence. What were you going to say?" I demand.

She turns those gorgeous green eyes back up at me. The look she gives me is so obviously troubled, I know something is definitely up.

"I can't tell you," she breathes. "It's unprofessional."

Her lip slides between her teeth again. *Jesus fucking Christ, she cannot know how sexy that is.*

"Laney." I lean forward, until my face is inches from hers. "I know you don't exactly fuckin' trust me. I know you don't wanna do the wrong thing here. And I get that you've got professional obligations and shit. But I think you wanna do the right thing by Paisley. And so do I." I pause. "Sometimes, the right thing to do is different from what everyone else is tellin' you you're supposed to do."

She shakes her head, her eyes glancing away from mine. She doesn't say anything for a few seconds. But I'm waiting her out, and I'm not taking no for an answer.

Finally, she sighs.

"I hope I don't regret this," she murmurs. "But there's something else the doctor found when Paisley was brought in."

A gainst my better judgment, I end up telling Rourke about the bruise Doctor Methaney noticed on Paisley's arm.

When the meaning of my words sinks in, Rourke's face transforms into a mask of pure fury. "Jesus fucking Christ," he hisses. "Are you tellin' me what I think you are?"

I nod. "I talked to Bethany about it. She said it happened the night before Paisley's fall. She swore it was the first time it's happened."

He stares at the wall, his features turning to stone. For a second, think he's going to punch it.

"I'm gonna fuckin' kill him."

Rourke doesn't shout the words. He speaks them quietly. Without any inflection. And somehow, they seem even more frightening that way.

"Rourke, please," I stammer. "Listen to me." My heart begins to pound.

"Ain't no more to be said." His jaw is clenched tight.

"Yes there is!" I retort, then stop myself. His face is an angry mask, and I know he's going to have trouble hearing anything I say right now. I need to do my best to exude calm through my voice.

"Rourke," I say softly, to get his attention. "Look at me. Please."

I wait, several seconds. Finally, his eyes flicker and turn to mine, dark as coals.

"First," I begin, "it doesn't make any sense for you to go to jail for hurting Mickey. He's not worth it. And that's what will happen if you beat him up here at the hospital. Okay?" I wait, but his features don't change. I try again. "And second — and more importantly — did you hear what I said before? Bethany kicked him out of the motel for hurting Paisley. Which means, she might be on the verge of being strong enough to leave him for good. If we can help her to be."

I stop for a moment, to let my words sink in.

"Not to get all social worker on you," I continue. "But on average, it takes a woman several attempts to successfully leave a toxic or abusive relationship. Bethany has clearly been caught up in this role with Mickey where she's supporting and taking care of him. It looks to me like she might be on the verge of breaking that cycle. The best way by far to help her get him out of the picture permanently is if she realizes once and for all — for herself — that he's not worth her time." I pause. "If you hurt Mickey now, it might actually backfire. Bethany might let her guilt and caretaker tendencies come roaring back, and feel like she has to stay with him longer." I take a deep breath and let it out. "Does that make sense?"

"Not if I actually kill him."

"Rourke, stop joking," I say, not at all sure that's what he's doing.

"Fuck!" he rasps. Suddenly, he pounds his fist on the table, hard enough to make the other customers in the coffee shop jump in their chairs. One of them scurries up out of her chair and quickly leaves the shop.

"This is fucking bullshit," he seethes. "That motherfucker needs be out of the picture."

"I don't disagree." I wrap both hands around my coffee cup for comfort and keep my voice steady. "I wish there was something we could do to keep Mickey away from Bethany and Paisley, long enough for Bethany to really feel how much easier her life is without him. It's pretty obvious he's a petty thief, to say the least. That can't be good for Paisley to be around." I blow out a disgusted breath. "Do you know, he was trying to get morphine from the nurses the other day?"

"He what?" Rourke grunts, expression still stormy.

"That's right." I almost have to laugh at the memory. "It was the day after Paisley was brought in. He said they wanted to take her home, and the nurses should give him her painkillers so he could give it to her himself. To 'save money'."

"He said that?" Despite how angry Rourke is, this news seems to pull him back into the present a little. He actually snorts at my words. "That guy's ballsy as well as stupid as shit, I'll give him that."

"Do you think he wanted the for himself?" I ask. "Or to sell?"

"To sell, most likely," he growls. "From what I hear, he's the kind of guy who's always looking for anything he can beg, borrow or steal and make a profit on. Drugs would be an easy first choice. And what better place but a hospital..." Rourke trails off. "Shit," he mutters.

"What?"

"I think I have an idea." Rourke says slowly, his brow furrowing. "Ya know, I saw Mickey here the other day, fiddling with a locked door. Trying to get it open. At the time I didn't know what he was tryin' to pull. But now I'm guessin' he was looking for shit to steal."

I look at him, stupefied. "Here at the hospital? Are you serious?" God, what a total dirtbag this guy is. "I wish we could catch him in the act," I say with a sigh of frustration. "That would be the perfect excuse to get him banned from here."

"Yeah," he says. "Exactly."

"What?"

For the first time since I told him about Paisley's bruise, the hint of a grin plays across Rourke's face.

"We catch him in the act," he says simply. "Or rather, we set him up so that the right people catch him. We get him not just banned from the hospital. If we play our cards right, we get him out of the picture completely. At least for a few days, and maybe even longer."

"You can't be serious!" I protest after Rourke has explained his plan that's started to form in his head.

"Why not?" he shrugs. "You don't want me to give him a beat-down. This is a way to get him out of the picture for a while."

"But it's... it's crazy!"

"What's crazy about it?" he challenges me. "This is a hospital. There's drugs all over the goddamn place. All we gotta do is make it easy for Mickey to get caught in the act trying to steal some. He gets hauled off, spends a few days in the slammer waiting for charges. Assuming no one posts bail, he's out of Bethany's hair. And away from Paisley."

"But I don't see how we actually make it work."

"It can't be that complicated," he counters. "We just gotta lead the dipshit to water, and he'll drink, right? Ain't no way a loser like Mickey who's down on his luck and lookin' for a quick way to make a buck is gonna resist a golden opportunity that's right in front of him."

"It's not that simple. There's no real way he could get into the pharmacy. And all of the med cabinets and closets in the hospital are locked. Only authorized people have access."

"Right. So your job is to figure out how to get one unlocked, so Mickey can get caught with his hand in the cookie jar. I can take care of gettin' him caught."

"Stop mixing metaphors," I retort. "And *all* I have to do is make sure the med cabinet is unlocked?"

"You think you can handle it?" He leans forward, his dark eyes locking on mine.

"How?" I ask.

"You tell me."

I blink, and sit back in my chair, thinking.

"I don't know that I can," I say slowly. "Only medical staff have access to the Pyxis machine that dispenses meds. A nurse or doctor has to log in with their credentials and input the patient before they can get drugs out. As a social worker, I don't have authorization. The only way I can think of to trap Mickey would be to make it easy for him to steal someone else's credentials and clear out the machine."

"So, let's do that."

"It's not that simple," I protest. "Even if he was caught red-handed, the person whose credentials he took would register as having unlocked the machine. They would be immediately under suspicion, either for being involved or for failing to keep track of their ID." I shake my head. "I can't put any of the hospital employees at risk like that. I think we have to think of another way."

Rourke frowns, then nods. "Okay. I see your point. So, there's gotta be something else he can steal around here that'd be easier to get at."

"I mean, technically, there's plenty of stuff, if you're looking. But, how would we trick him into doing it? And doesn't that mean we have to let him actually *steal* something?" I fret. "I'm not sure I'm comfortable with that. Supposing he gets away?"

"He won't," Rourke smirks. "I know a guy on the police force."

"Wait, what? *You* are friends with a police officer?" I say, amazed. "Now I've heard everything."

Rourke laughs. "We went to school together. We ain't buddies or anything exactly, but... yeah. I'm pretty sure I could get him to just coincidentally be here at the hospital when he needs to be."

"So... your plan is to actually get Mickey arrested." Now it's my turn to be amused.

"Yeah. Hell, it's not like my cop friend is gonna say no to arresting someone who actually commits a crime, right? Joe can put the guy in a cell for a few days. Until Paisley is out of the hospital, probably longer. No way Mickey'll be able to post bail, right."

"And after that?"

"After he gets out, I'll make it so Mickey understands it's in his best interests to stay the hell away from that little girl and her mom." His eyes gleam. "And Ironwood. And southern Ohio, while we're at it."

From the determined look one Rourke's face, I have no doubt he's dead serious about all of this. I shake my head in grudging admiration. "Unbelievable."

"But it'll work. I'll make sure it does." He gives me a conspiratorial grin. "So, what do you say? You in?"

13

LANEY

There's a little voice inside me saying, *This is crazy, Laney. Don't do it. Don't get involved. You could risk your job.* And for a second, I listen to it.

But the thing is, there's another voice that's louder. And that one says: The only way that little girl is going to be safe is if Mickey goes away.

It's better if Bethany doesn't suspect anything. I know she kicked him out once, but he came right back. Who knows how long it will be until she has the courage and the strength to get rid of him for good? And what could happen to the woman and her daughter in the meantime?

I feel a little guilty for interfering in their lives. But knowing she's already tried to get rid of him once makes it seem a little less bad.

Besides, Mickey will only get caught if he actually does try to steal something. Right?

"I'll think about it," I say slowly. "And if I can figure out a way to make this work, then... yes. I'll do it."

"Really?" Rourke raises a brow.

"Yes, really," I shoot back, a little defiantly. "You didn't think I would?"

"Honestly? No. I didn't." The corners of his lips tilt upward.

"Then why did you ask me?"

"Because doing it with your help would be easier than doing it without."

Am I crazy? I ask myself as Rourke looks at me with an impressed smile. *Have I lost my mind, here?* My heart starts to race as I contemplate what I'm planning to do. I realize I'm stepping over a line right now. A line I can't cross back over once I've done it.

I'm not sure how I got here. But somehow, I still know that if I could replay the last thirty minutes, I'd end up in the same place. I know I'm not going to back out.

"I want Mickey out of Paisley and Bethany's life," I say simply. "And I know in my heart, both of them want him gone, too." I suck in a deep, shaky breath. "And honestly, if this way stops you from beating Mickey senseless in the parking lot and going to jail yourself," I say, trying to sound like I'm joking, "then I'm in."

He leans forward some more, until his face is just inches from mine. "Don't do this for me, Laney," he warns in a low murmur. "I'm not asking you for that."

The sound of my name in his mouth makes goosebumps pucker the skin of my arms. This is the first time he's called me just by my name alone — not *Laney the social worker*, or *hey you*, or even *darlin'*.

The deep rasp of his voice is almost intimate. Almost like a caress from his rough, callused hands.

"I'm not doing it for you," I say, looking down. But I'm not sure if it's the truth.

"Promise me," he insists. He reaches across the table and puts a finger under my chin, lifting my face up toward his.

The contact, unexpectedly electric, jolts me. Startled, I look up just as his eyes lock on mine.

Iron Will 97

In them is an expression I've never seen from him, or from any other man. It's got nothing to do with what we've been talking about for the last fifteen minutes.

It's *hunger*. A desire so raw, so immediate, it shakes me to my core.

In his eyes, I see all of my own desire reflected back at me.

Every thought I've had about his hands on my body, late at night as I lie in the dark.

Every dream I've woken from, my skin crying out to be touched.

Every time I've whispered his name as I find my release, slick fingers between my legs — and then told myself I need to stop thinking about him, even though it's just a fantasy.

When he withdraws his hand, I'm trembling.

"Rourke," I half-whisper, my unsteady voice betraying me. "I'm doing it for everyone. If you hurt him here at the hospital, people will see it." I shake my head. "You'll go to jail. And Mickey won't. And he'll still be with Paisley's mom, and there won't be anything we can do about it. You won't have done them any good at all."

His jawline hardens. "I'm gonna enjoy fucking this guy over," he growls.

"Fine. But you're right: if there's a good way to do it, it's this one."

How is it that suddenly, trapping Mickey into trying to steal from the hospital seems like the *sane* course of action?

Rourke closes his eyes for a second, his jaw still tense. When he opens them again and looks at me, I see all the force of the emotions he's trying to contain within himself.

"Tell me something, Laney the social worker," he rasps. "Doesn't it eat at you? Shit like this?"

"Yes," I admit softly. "It does. I see a lot of things that really get to me. That make it hard to sleep at night, sometimes." I let out a ragged breath. "But often, those cases are the ones where the course of action is clear. Where I don't have to question what the best thing to do is. The worst cases for me— the hardest ones — are when both of the parents are unfit. It's hard to know what to do in cases like that. To know at what point a child would be better off being removed from their family." I shake my head. "At least here, we know Bethany loves Paisley. She's just in a tough situation. There's hope."

I stare into Rourke's glinting eyes. Maybe I should be afraid of him. But more than anything, I'm filled with admiration at how much he seems to care about this young girl.

"Why'd you decide to be a social worker?" he demands.

My mind is starting to reel with all these sudden changes of subject. "Why do you ask?"

His expression is unreadable. "You don't seem like the type."

Despite my confusion, I have to smile. "What does that mean? What does a social worker look like?"

"The ones I've met?" He scoffs. "Tired. Old. Prematurely gray."

"How many social workers have you met?"

"No changing the subject," he says gruffly. "I asked you a question."

"I, um..." I hesitate. "Well, I guess it was the combination of a lot of things."

I take a sip of my coffee, considering how much I should tell him.

"When I was a little girl," I say, "I had this friend. Emma. Her parents were abusive to her. I didn't really know the full extent of it at the time. I just knew that her mom was mean. And that whenever I'd see them together at school or something, my friend always looked really scared."

Thinking back to that time, my stomach starts to hurt, even all these years later.

"One day, she didn't show up to school. That in itself wasn't that unusual. She skipped a lot, for whatever reason. But then she didn't show up the next day, either. I remember that was a Friday. Because after that was the weekend. And I just figured she'd have to be back on Monday, you know?"

I swallow painfully. "Well, Monday came. And when I got to school, I remember that almost right away, it felt like something was... *wrong*. Something I couldn't quite figure out. But all the teachers and other adults were acting really strange. They were usually so smiley and friendly. But that morning their faces looked weird. Like they were trying to look normal, but just couldn't do it.

"When the bell rang and we were all sitting at our desks, our teacher sat on a stool in the front of the room. She look at us all, one by one. And then she told us that Emma was dead. She said there had been an accident, and that Emma had gotten hurt really bad. She left it as vague as possible, on purpose, I'm sure. So in my mind, I pictured a car accident or something." I shake my head. "But you know, kids hear adults talking, when they think they're alone. And a group of us kids heard some teachers whispering about it after school a couple of days later. It turned out, Emma's mom had beaten her so badly that she died in the hospital from the injuries."

"Jesus Christ," Rourke mutters.

"So, my parents..." I continue, bitterness seeping into my voice. "Let's just say, they're well-off people. Very prominent in the community. When they heard about it, their reaction... well, it sickened me. Even at my young age. See, I had been friends with Emma for a while. But after the first time I brought her over to my house to play, my mom said I wasn't allowed to have her over anymore. She was too poor. Her family wasn't good enough for me to be friends with."

Anger surges through me at the memories resurface as I continue.

"And when Emma died? They didn't console me, or try to help me through it. No. Instead, my parents pulled me out of that public school. They enrolled me in a private academy. To keep me away from that kind of riff-raff in the future."

I turn and stare at Rourke. His features are tense, jaw pulsing. But he doesn't say a word. He just lets me keep talking.

"Years later — when I was in college and sort of hating the pressure my parents were putting on me to make me into a carbon copy of them — I got to be good friends with a girl who lived a floor below me in the dorms. She told me about her childhood. About how her dad was an alcoholic and physically abusive, and how a social worker had helped her mom and sisters escape from him. For some reason, her story made me think about Emma." I lift one shoulder. "I guess it just triggered something in me. I went to the School of Social Work the next day and asked for an appointment with an advisor. And the rest is history."

"How did your parents feel about that?"

I snort. "They're still pissed about it, to this day. They have no idea what I'm doing, or why I'm doing it. They're furious that they spent all that money on tuition — thinking they were essentially sending me to finishing school, so I could marry a nice, prominent rich guy. Instead, it turned me into a reprobate."

He lets out a short bark of laughter. "You're hardly a reprobate, Laney."

"It's all relative," I tell him with a smirk. "I'm the black sheep of my family. To them, I may as well be selling myself on the street."

"Your parents are that big a deal, huh?" He lets out a low whistle.

"You have no idea," I say drily. "Fortunately, my younger sister is more than happy to be the good little girl I wasn't. And she just got engaged, so I'm hoping maybe that will take some of the pressure off." I glance up at the clock on the far wall. "Shoot, I'd better go," I say apologetically. "I've got a mountain of work to do and I've already taken twice as long as I should have on this break."

As uncomfortable as I was a few minutes ago, now I'm sorry to end the conversation. Thankfully, Rourke looks much calmer now. And he's an oddly good listener. I stand and pick up my cup.

"Shouldn't this count as work?" he suggests, gesturing. "We were talking about a patient, right?"

I laugh. "We were basically talking about breaking the law. Not sure that counts."

"There's the law, and then there's doing the right thing. You're just letting Mickey suffer the consequences of his actions." Rourke says, standing as well.

The shop is deserted now, the few customers having left during our conversation. Even the barista is gone from behind the counter, probably in the back doing something.

I turn toward the milk and cream station, leaning over to deposit my coffee cup in the bin next to it.

When I swivel back around, Rourke is there, less than a foot away from me. So close I imagine I can feel the heat of his body on my skin.

At least I think it's my imagination.

"I..." I begin, and stop. I don't know what to say without calling attention to the fact that Rourke is close enough to kiss me. I look up at him, uncertain.

But then I don't have to say anything at all.

Because his mouth is on mine.

The taste of him makes me dizzy. I feel myself falter, but then his arm is around my waist. His other hand moves behind my head, his fingers sliding up to my hair. The kiss deepens, awakening a hunger deep inside me that's barely contained as I kiss back, my body making its own decisions as my brain takes a back seat. I've *never* been kissed like this before — it goes all the way through me, reaching every nerve ending, every cell, waking them all up until my whole body is yielding to his. He pulls me closer against him, and the hardness of his length pressing against me rips a moan of longing from my throat.

When he breaks the kiss, I've all but forgotten where I am.

"You're really something, Laney the social worker," he rumbles.

The sound of someone clearing their throat interrupts us.

Turning my head toward it, I see Blake Barber standing just outside the coffee shop.

His eyes travel from Rourke to me, narrowing as they do. He lifts up an arm and taps his finger on an imaginary watch on his wrist, then stalks away.

"I... uh..." I stammer. "I better..."

Rourke chuckles low in his throat. "What an asshole that guy is. Come on. I'll walk you back."

Less than a minute later, we're standing in front of my door. I'm still in a fog from the heat of his kiss.

Even though I'd be crazy to consider it after Blake just caught us, I'm almost hoping Rourke follows me into my office. But suddenly, he's all business.

"I'll be in touch about the plan," he tells me gruffly. "I gotta go talk to my cop friend. Meantime, if you see Mickey around here, let one of Lords standing guard outside Paisley's room know. I wanna have our guys keep track of that piece of shit while he's here."

I nod. "Okay."

"And let me know what times of day you see him here. If there's any patterns. I'll ask the Lords to do the same."

"Rourke," I murmur, "Can I ask you something?"

"What?"

His eyes meet mine, so deep I could drown in them.

"Why are *you* doing this?" I breathe. "I just told you about what made me decide to be a social worker. What makes you care so much about helping a little girl you don't even know?"

"I was one of those kids who needed a savior when I was little. I didn't get one." He pauses, and when he continues his voice is hard as steel again. "So I'll be damned if I'm gonna look the other way when I see someone in need of saving."

14

ROURKE

That chick Laney, man....

She is not what I thought she was.

I thought she was never gonna go for the plan to get Mickey out of the way. I was surprised as hell when it didn't take much to convince her. Even though I knew she was worried about Paisley, too.

But, then, I didn't know what Laney knew.

That piece of human filth has already hurt the little girl.

At first, I just wanted Mickey out of the picture. But now that it looks like the bruise they found on Paisley's arm comes from him, I want him to suffer.

A lot.

And I want him to know *why* he's suffering. Make it so he'll never even think about raising a hand to Paisley or any other little kid again.

If he even lives to make the decision.

But that's gonna have to come later. Right now, I got other shit to deal with. For now, we get him away from Paisley. Put him on ice. And hopefully give her mom some time to figure out that no worthless piece of shit like Mickey King is worth putting her daughter at risk.

I've never understood why the hell women stay with guys who don't treat them right. But damned if I don't know plenty of them who do.

My own mom was one, after all.

Like I told Laney, I was a kid who needed a savior when I was little. But saviors didn't exist for me back then.

So I had to save myself. Me, and my kid sister.

And I'll be damned if I let Paisley suffer the same fate.

I wonder whether shit would have been easier for me and Regan when we were kids if we'd had a social worker like Laney. Someone who actually gave a damn about us. Someone who would have tried to go to bat for us.

One thing's for sure, though. If Delaney Hart been my social worker back in the day, I would have been beating my meat thinking about her every damn night.

My cock is hard as a bat as I ride out of the hospital parking lot, savoring the memory of the way her lips melted under mine. Fuck, I didn't even really *decide* to kiss her. All of a sudden, I just *was*.

Hell, if it wasn't for that pussy-ass hospital administrator interrupting us, I'd probably be balls-deep inside her in her tiny little office right now.

Jesus. I can almost feel her warm, wet pussy around my aching cock.

It's been a couple of weeks since I last fucked anyone. That must be some kind of record for me. There's no particular reason for it, really. Just that the girls who like to hang around the club-house aren't really doing it for me these days. The same old overly made-up faces, the same old fake-ass tits… as hot as some of them are, they just don't hold my interest anymore.

That's why, instead of heading to the clubhouse from the hospital, I decide to just go home instead. As soon as I'm in my house, I go to the kitchen, pour myself a shot of whiskey, and settle in on the couch.

In a matter of seconds, I'm back at the hospital in my mind. When I knock on Laney's door, she looks up and sucks that pillow-soft lower lip between her teeth.

My cock strains against my zipper. I pull it out and start to stroke, as slowly as I can stand it. My dick's been hard for the last half-hour, and I can't take much more.

The office door is locked now. Laney's stripping for me, wriggling out of that tight little pencil skirt she was wearing today. She keeps the heels on, though. In my imagination, she's wearing a lacy little barely-there pair of panties under that skirt, the crotch soaking wet because she's been waiting for me. One by one, she undoes the buttons of her blouse, then tosses it on the chair. Her bra goes next. She unclasps the back, and they fall loose and free, the nipples rosy and hard as pebbles.

My strokes get faster.

Laney kneels in front of me. She looks up at me through her dark lashes, her eyes never leaving my face. She wraps those soft lips around me, taking my cock as deep as she can stand it. Her mouth is warm and wet as she starts to suck, moaning softly while she reaches up to pinch her nipples.

Jesus fuck, I can't hold out. With a shout, I unload in her mouth, coming hard and fast in thick, ropy strands. When I'm finished, I see stars.

Holy shit. It's been a while since I've come that hard.

If it feels this good just thinking about her, imagine what the real thing would be like.

Laney Hart, you've gotten inside my head.

And if the way you moaned when I kissed you today is any indication, it's only gonna be a matter of time before I get inside your panties.

THE NEXT DAY, I make a quick run over to talk to Joe McBride at the Ironwood police station.

Officer Joe McBride has been on the police force here in town for almost as long as I've been a Lord of Carnage. The two of us were buddies in high school. After that, let's just say we both headed in different directions. Joe's even married now, if you can believe that shit. He's got twin daughters, probably about four years old or so, I'm guessing. Last I heard, his wife Peggy is pregnant again.

Joe's a good cop. By which I mean he's good at his job, not particularly corrupt, and probably could have made it as a detective or something in a much bigger PD in a much bigger city. But he's a small town guy at heart, and he likes it here in Ironwood. Hell, I can't say I blame him. The Lords of Carnage have based both our chapters in small towns, to keep our operations more off the radar, and that suits me just fine.

When I get to the PD, I park my bike toward the back of the lot and walk inside. The cop behind the front desk does a double take when he sees me, but I ignore that shit.

"Hey. Joe McBride on duty?"

The cop frowns. "There a reason you need to see him?" he challenges.

"Yeah," I growl. "I wanna ask him to be my fuckin' Valentine. Just get him out here."

The guy looks like he wants to punch me but doesn't dare. He gets up and disappears through a steel door. A couple minutes later, Joe comes out through another locked door off to one side.

"Hey," he greets me with a smirk. "Just as much of an asshole as always, I see."

"Your front desk help needs some work on his fuckin' manners," I grunt. That gets a laugh out of Joe. "Look, I got somethin' I want to run by you. You got a few minutes?"

Joe gives me a brief nod. "I'm finishing some stuff up, but you wanna meet me outside in about five?"

"Yeah. Probably better that way, anyway."

Joe gives me a look of suspicion. "What kind of shit are you tryin' to get me messed up in, man?"

"Nah. It's nothing like that. At least, not exactly." I grin. "I think you might even enjoy this." I flip my thumb toward the entrance. "I'll be across the street."

I go outside and cross over to a small, deserted park, taking a seat on top of a paint-chipped picnic table. Joe joins me there a few minutes later.

"Okay," he grunts, taking a seat on the opposite end. "What the fuck is so important you need to bother me at work?"

I reach for my smokes and offer him one. "A couple things. First, what do you know about a loser named Mickey King? Ever heard of him?"

Joe looks down at the pack, hesitating. "Peggy doesn't like it when I smoke."

"Yeah. It's a filthy habit." I don't put them away, and after a second, Joe snorts and takes one. I hand him my lighter.

"Yeah, I've heard of Mickey King," he says, taking a long drag. "Jesus, that tastes good. Fuck these cancer sticks anyway. So, Mickey. We've brought him in a couple times for various things. Usually drunk and disorderly. I think he's got a couple other things on his record, too. Petty theft, from a while back. Oh, yeah, he did..."

Joe trails off. His face closes off, turns 'cop neutral.'

"What?" I demand. Something tells me he just remembered something about Mickey that makes him more interesting to him than he's willing to tell me.

"Nothing."

"Fuck it, Joe," I complain. "You really gonna bust my balls on this?"

"Look, man," Joe shoots back. "I don't know why you think I have some obligation to tell you shit. You're lucky I don't go lookin' around in your club's business. You oughta leave well enough alone."

I ignore him. "What if I told you you could nab Mickey on a drug charge?" I suggest. "If I could hand him to you on a platter?" I wait a beat, until I can see he's considering it. "I bet that fucker would sing like a bird about anything and everything he knows, if he thought you could put him in county for a good long time."

Joe's jaw works as he thinks about my words. "Why would you do that? Did he run afoul of the Lords or something?"

"Not exactly," I shake my head. "He ran afoul of me, though. And someone I'm trying to protect."

I let Joe ask me a couple more questions, just to show him I'm on the up and up. Then, when I can tell I've got him on the hook, I tell him about my plan. At first he doesn't look like he's gonna go for it. But when I explain why I'm doing this, his face grows dark. Like I said, he's got two little girls at home.

"Why would I just happen to be at the hospital at the precise moment when he's trying to steal drugs ?" he asks skeptically.

I shrug. "Does it matter? Say you're visiting your Aunt Matilda or something. No one's gonna be asking why a cop is anywhere, Joe."

He waits a couple more seconds. Finally, he pulls on the last drag of his cigarette and stubs it out on the table next to him. "I wouldn't mind putting the fear of God into that little shit."

I can see by the gleam in his eye he'll be getting more out of it than that, but I don't push it. I don't give a rat's ass what he does with that peckerwood, as long as he puts the asshole behind bars for a while.

"So you'll do it?"

"Sure." He smiles for the first time. "I ain't been over to the hospital for a while. Maybe I will visit my Aunt Matilda after all."

"Good deal. I'll figure the details out, and get you down there in time to catch him in the act."

"That it?" Joe starts to stand.

"One more thing," I say, stopping him. "What do you know about the cops down in Louisville? You know any precincts there with a reputation for being on the take by anyone? Any gangs or syndicates?"

Joe furrows a brow. "I don't know much about shit down there. I've heard bits here and there, but nothing really useful. Why?"

"No reason," I tell him, keeping my face expressionless.

Joe snorts. "Yeah, right. But you know what? I'm gonna let it go that you asked me that question, because I do *not* want to know."

"Probably better that way," I agree.

I didn't expect to find out much from Joe about whether any PDs in Louisville are in the pocket of rivals to the Dos Santos cartel. But it was worth a shot, anyway.

I tell Joe I'll be in touch, and we part ways. He goes back into the building, and I head back to my bike.

15

LANEY

I don't see or hear from Rourke for a couple of days after that. It's long enough that I'm not sure whether he's forgotten about our plan.

Paisley is doing better and better all the time. The bruises on her face are healing, and her headaches are getting less frequent and severe. The break of her arm is a clean one, fortunately, and Doctor Methaney tells me he doesn't think she'll have any problems with it once it heals.

This is all great news, but it presents a problem. It's getting harder and harder to keep her here and safe from Mickey.

I track down Doctor Methaney as he's just getting off a shift in surgery. Kent Methaney is an attractive middle-aged gay man with kind eyes. His husband is a local lawyer, whom I've never actually met but have seen around town. He is aware of Paisley's situation, and he's been more than willing to keep her here as long as possible, to help me stall for time. But today when I talk to him, his eyes are somber.

"I think I'm nearing the end of what I can reasonably do to avoid discharging Paisley," he murmurs as we walk down the hall together. "I can't lie on the charts. And to be honest, Barber is really starting to breathe down my neck about this." Kent reaches up and massages his neck with his hand in an unconscious gesture. "There's no other way you can protect Paisley?"

"I'm working on it," I say. "But I don't want to try to go after the boyfriend through the system right now. There's not enough evidence of harm, and unfortunately, it would just hurt Paisley and her mom in the end. Can we just keep her here one more day?" I plead.

He sighs. "Yes. One more day. But after that, Laney, there's nothing more I can do."

HALF A DOZEN TIMES, I want to go down to Paisley's room and ask the Lords standing outside how I can get hold of Rourke. But my pride always stops me. Which brings me face to face with an uncomfortable truth. I need to talk to him about the plan to get Mickey away from the little girl and her mother for a few days. But that's not the main reason I want to talk to him.

The main reason is because I want to look in his eyes, and see whether he's forgotten about what happened between us in the coffee shop.

God, I am *ridiculous*. I can't help but groan in frustration at myself. I should just be focusing on getting Bethany help. And I should definitely forget that anything ever happened between Rourke and me. But that's a lot easier said than done. I *hate* how many times I've thought of him since he kissed me. How many times I've fantasized about what might happen the next time I see him.

Less than a week ago, the mere idea that anything could ever happen between us would have made me laugh. The distance between us — between his world and mine — was too great for me to ever seriously imagine that anything could ever happen between us. Paradoxically, that made it feel safe to fantasize about him. He was unattainable, and therefore not exactly... *real*.

But now?

My body remembers the touch of his rough hands. The surprising softness of his mouth. The taste of him.

I remember his laugh. How surprised I was to hear it. It's been echoing in my mind ever since.

I've been longing to hear it again. Longing to feel the caress of his breath against my neck.

I shiver.

It's pathetic of me. God help me, he and I are from worlds about as different as two people's can be. But I can't deny it, as stupid as I am for letting myself feel it.

I wish he'd never kissed me. I wish he was still nothing more to me than a dangerously delicious fantasy. Something to occupy my nighttime fantasies.

Before, I was lusting after an *idea*. The hot, unattainable biker.

Now... I'm longing for the *man*.

FEELING like I'm turning around in circles, I decide to go pay Paisley a visit. I find her mom there with her, as well as one of the Lords — the one they call Yoda.

Paisley is busy coloring something on her cast with a packet of markers that's strewn out in front of her. She's wearing ear buds connected to a cell phone lying in front of her, bobbing her head in rhythm to a song only she can hear. Bunnifer sits placidly beside her. Yoda is half-perched in the well of the window beside the bed. Bethany is sitting in a chair across from him, laughing, her head thrown back.

"Hey, everyone," I greet them with a smile. Paisley immediately looks up and flashes me a wide grin of recognition.

"Hi, Laney!" she cries, the music making her talk louder. "Do you want to sign my cast?"

"Wow," I marvel, coming closer. "Are you sure there's even room?"

It's true. There are signatures and drawings covering practically ever inch of the space. Scrawls of all shapes and sizes. Judging from her cast, Paisley's the most popular girl in town.

"All the Lords signed it," she says proudly, holding it out. "Yoda drew this! I'm coloring it."

I have to laugh as I look more closely at the design. It's a picture of a little girl with long hair and a superhero cape. Paisley's only gotten as far as coloring her hair a vibrant shade of purple.

"That's totally cool!" I enthuse.

I pick up a green marker and find a rare bare spot on the plaster, then sign my name. As I cap the marker, I notice Rourke's signature a couple of inches away, and redden at the fact that it actually makes my stomach do a little flip.

Paisley goes back to coloring and listening to her music. I turn to the adults. "She seems like she's doing really well today."

"Thank God," Bethany sighs. "I've been so worried that the concussion would have longer lasting effects. I made the mistake of googling severe concussions, which led me to traumatic brain injuries..." She shudders. "I really feel like we dodged a bullet."

"She's tough," Yoda says. "Tough and beautiful. Like her mama."

Bethany looks down and blushes. "Flatterer," she murmurs.

"It ain't flattery if it's true, darlin'," Yoda grins.

Hmmm. *Interesting development.* The two of them seem like they're enjoying one another's company quite a bit.

"Oh!" exclaims Bethany, glancing at the phone on Paisley's bed. "I have to get going. I'll be late for work." She looks at Yoda with a shy smile. "You sure you don't mind taking me?"

"Havin' you on the back of my bike, darlin'?" he banters back. "Are you kiddin' me? That'd be any man's dream come true."

Bethany turns to me with a sour look. "Mickey took off with

my car," she explains. "The jerk. And he's not answering my texts to bring it back."

Bethany takes her phone from Paisley, who complains a little but doesn't fuss too much. She kisses her daughter on the forehead, and hands her the remote so she can watch TV.

"I'll be back after work, baby," she croons. "You need anything, you know you can call one of the nurses. And the Lords are right outside."

As I walk out of the room with the two of them, my own cell phone buzzes in the pocket of my blazer. I pull it out to see my sister is calling. I wave goodbye to Yoda and Bethany and turn in the direction of my office as I answer it.

"Hey, Linds."

"That's the future Mrs. Harris to you," my sister jokes.

"So noted. Congrats, by the way."

"Thank you! Did you see the pictures of the venue I put on Instagram?"

"No, sorry," I reply, grimacing. "Haven't been on Instagram a lot lately."

'Well, I added them to my stories, so you can see them there."

"Great. I'll do that," I lie. I keep walking past my office, toward the atrium at the center of the building.

"So, anyway," she continues. "I'm calling to ask you a favor!" Her tone of voice sounds more like she's about to do *me* one. "I want to invite you to be one of my bridesmaids! Kelly and I are fighting because she called me a bridezilla, so I'm replacing her. Screw her, right?"

Kelly. I can call up a picture of her in my head right away. She and Lindsay have known each other since middle school. She's the mousiest of all Linds's friends — the girl just a little less stylish, a little less pretty than the others. It occurs to me to wonder whether my appearance-conscious sister might have been fretting about how Kelly would look in the wedding photos Lindsay will inevitably be posting on social media — and whether she's been looking for an excuse to kick her off the lineup, so to speak.

For just a second, I consider saying no. But she's my sister, after all. And besides, I'd never hear the end of it from either her or my mother if I declined.

I take a deep breath, squinching up my face at what I'm about to do. "Sure, I'd be happy to, Linds," I say.

"Great!" she chirps. "So, I'll add you to the group chat. If you could try to get up to speed pretty soon, that would be great. We're working on nailing down dates to go dress shopping right now."

"Will do," I mutter, already regretting my decision.

"Awesome! Oh, one more thing. I'm putting together my first draft of the guest list, and I wanted to know whether you want me to include a plus-one for you."

I've made a full circle around the atrium now, so I turn around and head back the other way. There's something in my sister's tone that tells me she's assuming I'm going to say no to the plus-one.

It occurs to me to be just a little bit offended. I mean, sure, I've been single for a while, but it's not *that* ridiculous to imagine me bringing a date, is it?

It would serve her right if I brought Rourke, I think, and have to suppress a bout of hysterical laughter. *God, just think of how much she and my parents would freak!*

"I'm not sure," I mumble, at once amused by the thought and horrified that I let myself be pathetic enough to think it. Rourke would probably sooner kill himself than go to a society wedding. And I can't say I blame him for that. Plus, I'd rather drive off a cliff than humiliate myself by asking him.

"Well, it's still super early, anyway," my sister replies cheerfully. "I'll just put down no, and you can tell me if that changes."

"Sure."

My sister chats away for a few more minutes, but at this point

I'm barely listening to her. By the time she ends the call, I'm slumped in one of the uncomfortable couches near the hospital entrance. As I lower my phone from my ear, I imagine myself months from now, at Lindsay's fancy blowout of a wedding. Instead of doing my best to stay out of the limelight, now I'll be front and center as a bridesmaid.

I already know the judgments that will swirl around me. The gossip mill that bored rich women love to feed with their speculations and fake sympathies. I know I'll be the subject of many conversations that night, even as they all pretend to be focusing on my sister and her happy future.

It won't matter to any of them that this is a life I've chosen for myself. That I'm happy where I am, doing what I'm doing. All they'll see is that I'm dateless and out of place. They will politely ask me about my life, then whisper behind my back about how sad it is that Senator Hart's older daughter is still single, and working at some awful job in some town no one's ever heard of — without even a plus-one to bring to her own sister's wedding.

16

LANEY

"Paisley is set to leave the hospital tomorrow," I tell Rourke over the phone.

Just when I was at the point of breaking down and begging the Lords for Rourke's number, he finally called me on my office phone.

"I can't get the doctor to keep her here any longer," I continue. "Blake is breathing down his neck about it. As well as mine."

"So we're running out of time."

I nod, even though Rourke can't see me. "Yes."

"Okay. Time to put the plan in place, then. We'll get Mickey nabbed tomorrow. I need to talk to my guy, let him know when to be there. Can you get me an ETA on when Paisley's gonna be discharged?"

"Mid-morning, probably," I say. "And I know from Bethany that Mickey has taken her car from her. Which is shitty for her, but a stroke of luck for us, because he'll have to be here to drive them home." I scowl. "Unless he's too much of a pig to even bother to show up, that is."

"We'll worry about that bridge if and when we come to it. For now, let's just move to get the plan in place."

I grin at the phone. "Operation Mouse Trap is on schedule for tomorrow, then."

"Cheesy," Rourke deadpans.

I start to reply, then my jaw drops as I realize what he just said.

"Did you just make a *joke*?" I marvel. "Wow, that was even worse than mine."

"I'll deny it to my grave," he tells me. "Look, I gotta go. Got some club business to attend to. But I'll see you tomorrow morning."

"Okay." My grin fades. "I hope this works."

"It will." There's no doubt in his voice. "Don't worry, darlin'. We got this."

"I CAN'T BELIEVE I let you talk me into this," Katie mutters. "It's insanity, you know that?"

I don't answer, because she has a point.

"We could both lose our jobs," she continues.

"Not as long as we don't get caught," I reassure her. "And we won't."

It had taken three margaritas at our favorite Mexican place — on my tab — to convince Katie to help us with the plan to nab Mickey. Luckily, Mickey has been such an asshole to all of the nurses, too — especially Katie — that the prospect of paying him back eventually won her over. I felt a little guilty about plying my best friend with alcohol to get her on board, but I'm trying not to think about that now.

"Are you totally sure your biker isn't setting you up?" Katie stops in the hallway, hands on her hips, and gives me a piercing look.

An unfortunate side effect of using alcohol to achieve my objective is that I was drinking, too — and in the process, I *may* have told Katie about Rourke kissing me in the coffee shop. Ever since, she has been referring to him as *your biker*.

To say I regret confiding in my best friend about this is an understatement at this point.

"Okay, first of all, for the last time, he's not *my* biker," I retort, feeling a flush of heat rise to my cheeks. "And second of all, that makes no sense. Why would Rourke be setting me up? He wants Mickey out of the picture as much as we do."

The plan isn't perfect, but it was the best we could come up with on short notice. Rourke put a tail on Mickey so we'd know right away the next time he showed up at the hospital. Since he's still got Bethany's car, it was relatively easy for the Lords to keep track of him, though I'm not exactly sure how they did it. Apparently, Rourke just got the call that he's on his way here now.

The most important thing was making sure that Paisley and Bethany are safe, and that they have no idea it's a set-up. We had to figure out a way to make Mickey walk right into the trap, without anyone else potentially getting hurt. And I think we've done that — even though anyone who bothered to think about it for very long would probably realize the whole thing sounded fishy.

Luckily, Mickey's not the sharpest tool in the shed.

Rourke's made sure that the Lords who normally stand guard outside Paisley's room are gone this morning when Mickey shows up. I just happen to be paying her and Bethany a visit when he arrives. He gives me a sharp, defiant look when he sees me sitting at the foot of Paisley's bed. When I don't say anything, he sneers and turns to Bethany.

"When she getting out?" he asks, gesturing at Paisley.

"I guess in an hour or so," Bethany tells him, giving me a furtive glance. "The doctor has been to see her this morning already. They're getting her paperwork finished up, and the nurse is supposed to be in with some painkillers for her to take home with her."

Right on schedule, Katie strolls into the room. She gives Mickey a sour glance, but like me, she doesn't challenge his being here. "All right, Paisley," she says breezily, smiling at the little girl. "We're almost ready to get you out of here. I just have to go grab you some pills for Mom to give you if anything starts to hurt too bad." She shakes her head and starts her performance.

"Getting meds for patients sure has changed," she murmurs as she grabs Paisley's chart and pretends to check some things off. "It used to be everything was all out in the open for us in a cabinet, to grab whatever we wanted. Now, we've got this machine that's sort of like a vending machine. It's great, though, don't get me wrong! It's got pretty much every painkiller and every type of med you need. All I have to do is log in and put in my fingerprint, and it opens right up! It's all right there! Whatever you need, right in front of you! It's pretty slick! Sure makes my life easier!"

I stare at the wall, struggling not to react or make eye contact. *Don't lay it on too thick, Kate,* I silently beg her in my head.

"So, I'm gonna go down there and grab you what you need, honey," she finishes, nodding at all of us. "I'll be back in just a bit."

Katie exits the room, strolling away so casually I almost laugh — except I'm far too nervous to find this very funny.

For about ten seconds, Mickey doesn't react. My stomach sinks as I start to think he's not going to take the bait.

But then, just as I'm about ready to lose hope, he pushes himself off the wall he's been leaning against.

"I'm gonna go take a leak," he announces.

Mickey strides out of the room. A couple of seconds later, there's a light tap at the door and Yoda comes in. He makes brief eye contact with me, then turns to Paisley and Bethany.

"So, sounds like someone gets to go home today!" he grins at the little girl. "You excited?"

"Yeah," she nods, lifting a shoulder. "Except I don't want to go back to school."

"Aw, but you have that cool cast, now," Yoda admonishes her. "You look like a bada—... like a real tough chick. You could tell the kids at school you got it by beating up a bad guy or something."

Paisley giggles, ducking her head. "That's lying!"

I listen to Yoda banter back and forth with Paisley and her mom. Minutes pass. Or maybe they're seconds, I don't know. I start to get more and more anxious. Now that Yoda's here, keeping an eye on the two of them, I'm suddenly a bundle of nerves — practically jumping out of my skin, wanting to know what's happening with Mickey.

I sit there as long as I can stand it. Then, abruptly, I stand up.

"I just wanted to check in with you two on my way to my office," I say, casually. "I'll be back in time to say goodbye to you, Paisley, okay?" I shoot a look at Bethany. "I'm still working on getting you some financial help for Paisley's stay. I just want you to know I haven't forgotten."

"Thank you," Bethany says gratefully. "I really appreciate it."

I go out into the hallway — dying to turn toward the wing with the med closet, but wanting to be as inconspicuous as possible. I wander to the closest restroom, wash my hands, come back outside, grab a drink at the drinking fountain. All the while, I'm trying to act nonchalant, but my nerves are jangling. *Is it over yet? Did Mickey go without a fight? Or did they not catch him? Is it possible he didn't take the bait — that he really did leave just to go to the bathroom?*

Maybe Mickey's smarter than he seems. Maybe he suspected we were trying to set him up, somehow. If so, that could mean Katie's in danger. *Should I go check on her? Should I—*

It's at that moment, just when I'm starting to work myself into a real panic, that I hear the shouting. Mickey's unmistakeable voice resounds down the hall, followed by a loud crash, then more yelling.

"Fuck you, man! I didn't do nothin'! This is fucking *bullshit*, man! I'll *kick* your ass!"

I join a rapidly forming group of curious people, now moving down the corridor in the direction of the noise. *Thank God for gawkers.* On the way, I pass Katie, heading in the other direction. As she passes me, she catches my eye, reaches out her hand, and gives me a low-five without stopping.

Rounding the corner is a uniformed police officer, about thirty years old, in good shape with just the beginnings of a receding hairline. He looks like Prince William, if Prince William packed on about thirty pounds of muscle and the beginnings of a dad bod. He's pushing a handcuffed Mickey in front of him, who's still struggling and yelling intermittently.

Belatedly, I realize I need to be acting like someone who doesn't know what's going on.

"What happened?" I call to the officer as he passes, loud enough for people to hear me ask.

"Just caught this guy breaking into one of the med dispensaries," he answers when he sees my hospital lanyard. Thankfully, we haven't met, so he has no idea I'm in on the whole thing. "Caught him in a scuffle with one of the nurses in a room with a med dispensary machine. He was stuffing fistfuls of Vicodin and anything else he could get his hands on into his pockets."

"It ain't what it looked like!" Mickey yells.

"Like hell it ain't," the cop says, pushing him forward. "You have the right to remain silent, you piece of shit, and I highly suggest for your own benefit you do so."

I barely manage to suppress my elated laughter as I watch the policeman continue to drag Mickey down the hallway. I lag about ten feet behind the rest of the crowd that's formed, biting back a smile.

My amusement is short-lived, though, when the door to Paisley's room opens. Bethany comes out just in time to watch her boyfriend being led away in cuffs. And of course, unlike me, she's not at all happy to see it.

"Mickey!" she cries out. "What's going on?"

"They're fuckin' arrestin' my ass!" he yells back. "You gotta get me out!"

"What for?" she cries. But the officer pushes him in the back again and tells him to shut up before Mickey can reply.

"You sit tight," I tell Bethany, feeling suddenly guilty. "Go in with Paisley. I'll be back in a second to tell you everything I can find out."

Yoda comes out of Paisley's room to lead her back inside. Reluctantly, Bethany goes with him. The officer pushes Mickey into the elevators, and I take the stairs down so I can honestly report back. I rush to the front entrance just in time to beat them there.

"Excuse me, officer," I say hurriedly. "This man's girlfriend has a child who's a patient here. What should I tell her about what happens next?"

The cop gives me an impassive look, then cocks his head. He seems to be considering whether to answer me, but his eyes flick down to my lanyard and badge. Finally, he shrugs. "I'm taking him down to the station to book him into the jail. There'll be a bond schedule, so he could pay right away to get out." His eyes glint with just a hint of amusement. "But I guarantee you, he can't afford it."

BACK UPSTAIRS, I find Yoda consoling Bethany, who's freaking out.

"What am I going to do?" she wails, distraught. "I don't have any money to get him out!"

For the first time, it occurs to me that it's possible we may have just added to her problems instead of helping her. Of course she'd feel like it's her job to bail Mickey out of jail. My stomach starts to churn as I worry this was all a big mistake.

But then Yoda speaks up.

"He got himself into this," he soothes her. "He can get his own self out. This ain't your problem, Bethany."

"But..."

"No buts. He's a grown-ass man." He glances at Paisley and winks. "Sorry about the bad word, sweetheart."

Paisley giggles. "It's okay."

"Mickey was coming to take us home," Bethany murmurs. "He's still got the keys to my car! I..."

"I'll get y'all home," Yoda says, interrupting her. "You'll be fine."

Bethany looks at him and smiles gratefully.

"Okay," comes a voice from the open doorway. We all turn to see Katie standing at the threshold. "Now that all the commotion is over, let's get Paisley discharged!"

I LEAVE THEM TO IT, promising Bethany I'll be in touch very soon. Then, sighing, I exit Paisley's hospital room, thankful things seem to have worked out okay, at least for now.

One thing seems odd, though. Rourke told me over the phone yesterday that he'd "see me tomorrow." I assumed that meant he'd be here to witness Mickey's takedown. I wonder if he's gotten held up somewhere — or whether I should have tried to call him when Mickey showed up here.

I realize with a sinking heart that I was looking forward to seeing him. Now that Mickey's taken care of, and Paisley will be leaving the hospital, it's very possible I might never run into Rourke Powers again.

I'm not proud of it, but I'm a lot more disappointed than I have any right to be.

I go back to my office and sit down at my desk to try to work. But the excitement of the last half-hour has my brain in a jumble. I spend the rest of the day idly surfing the net, looking at cat videos, and trying unsuccessfully to focus. This isn't like me; normally, I love my job, and I'm not much of a procrastinator, even for tasks I find uninspiring.

By the time five o'clock rolls around, I'm cranky, impatient, and nursing the beginnings of a headache. Frustrated, I push my laptop away from me and don't even consider taking any work home. I need a break.

As I walk out of the hospital entrance, I'm already trying to think of something more inspiring to do this evening than a load of laundry and a meal of leftovers. I don't even notice the lone figure leaning against the low brick wall separating the front walk from the decorative landscaping behind it.

"So," a familiar voice rumbles, startling me out of my thoughts. "Mission accomplished, I hear."

I laugh softly and turn toward Rourke.

"Mission accomplished," I smile.

"You in the mood to celebrate?"

A week ago — hell, even a few days ago — I wouldn't have even considered going somewhere alone with Rourke. But now, my stomach jumps with nervous excitement.

"Yeah," I answer, trying to ignore the shiver that runs down my spine when his eyes lock on mine. "Yeah, I really am."

17

LANEY

Rourke wants me to go with him on his bike, but one glance at the tailored straight skirt I'm wearing changes his mind.

"Head home and change," he directs me. "Give me your address and I'll be by in half an hour or so."

My pulse is thudding in my temples as I tell him where I live. "Where are we going?"

"You'll see." His eyes twinkle as they slide over my body. "Wear something you can ride in. If I didn't make that clear."

I'm fighting against nerves as I drive home to the tiny house I rent on the north side of Ironwood. I've never ridden on a motorcycle before. Hell, I've never even *touched* a motorcycle before. I have no idea what to wear, and I'm half-afraid I won't have the guts to climb on the back of a large, black machine like the one Rourke drives.

But as scared as I am, I push down my worry. Because I don't want Rourke to think I'm a ninny.

Figuring wherever Rourke is taking me won't be someplace high-end and snooty, I opt for my oldest, most casual jeans. They're the comfiest thing I own, but they also hug my butt and thighs in a way I know is flattering. A simple white T-shirt is next, and thankfully I have a leather jacket that's just casual enough, without looking like I'm trying too hard for a "biker chick" look. I start to pull on some high-heeled shoes, then rethink that and grab some booties with just a little bit of a heel.

When I look in the mirror, I'm suddenly filled with doubt. This seems crazy, to be going out with him. I mean, is this actually a date? Or a hookup? Or something else? I have no idea what I've just agreed to. I've never even seen Rourke outside of the hospital. I don't know what he expects of me — if he even expects anything at all.

I grab a ponytail holder and pull back my dark hair, hoping that way it won't get too tangled up in the wind. Then, since I still have a little time, I run to the bathroom and brush my teeth, then reapply some of my makeup. The doorbell rings just as I'm putting on fresh lipstick, and I jump and let out a little squeak of nerves. Laughing at myself, I stick out my tongue at my reflection.

"Calm down," I tell the woman in the mirror. "This is no big deal. You're just going out to have a good time. That's all."

Unfortunately, she doesn't look at all convinced.

ROURKE IS STANDING on the cement stoop when I open the front door. His large body practically fills the entire opening. He hasn't changed clothes or anything since I last saw him less than an hour ago. But somehow he looks different, outside the sterile environment of the hospital.

"You look good." A corner of his mouth tilts up. "You ready?"

Not trusting my voice, I nod and push open the screen door. I had the foresight to only bring a small crossbody purse, and after I've locked the door behind me, I drop my keys into it and follow Rourke down the small path to my driveway, where his motorcycle is parked.

"You ever ridden on the back of a bike before?" When I shake my head no, he doesn't look surprised. "I brought you a helmet. Here, put this on."

I'm taken aback by how heavy the object he hands me is. Fortunately, once it's on my head, I don't notice the weight so much. I fumble with the chin strap a bit, and Rourke reaches up and fastens it for me, adjusting it so it fits snugly but not too tight.

"Okay." He turns and straddles the bike, then lifts his chin to motion behind him. "Get on behind me, and put your feet on those pegs down there." I do as he tells me, noting nervously that there's no back rest behind me. What if I fall off backwards once the bike is moving?

The roar of the engine startles me and I jump in my seat, stifling a cry. In front of me, Rourke's body is shaking with mirth. "No need to be nervous," he calls out over the roar. "Put your arms around my waist."

For one long second, I consider climbing off the bike and running back into the house.

The bike doesn't move, and neither does Rourke. As though he knows to give me time.

Good God, Laney. Don't be such a baby. You spend your entire life either at the hospital or in this house. Live a little. Ride a motorcycle. Go somewhere unexpected with a handsome biker. Stop thinking so much. Just for tonight.

I lean forward and wrap my arms around Rourke.

There's a soft clunk as he puts the bike into gear. And then we start to move. Instinctively, my arms tighten around his waist. His abs are like steel. They barely yield as I squeeze like my life depends on it.

"Relax, babe," he says. "I got you."

For the first five minutes or so, I barely breathe, my muscles taut as rubber bands. It's as though my body thinks that if I relax, I'll die. But being that tense is exhausting, and eventually, my muscles start to surrender. Rourke weaves us in and out of traffic as we ride through town, and then we pass the city limits and head out into the countryside. Once we're out on the open road, I start to notice the fluid movements of the bike a little more. It's a little bit like being on a bicycle, except faster, of course. And more exciting.

As my muscles relax and I start to breathe more normally, I find myself almost enjoying the feel of the wind rushing by us, and the hypnotic thrum of the engine.

Not to mention the warmth of Rourke's body against mine.

I turn my head and watch the trees and fields fly by. The muscles underneath his shirt flex as Rourke negotiates the twists and turns. So much power in the motorcycle underneath us. So much raw strength in the man whose life is currently in my hands.

It's intoxicating.

I take a deep breath in, then exhale slowly, suddenly feeling more alive than I have in I don't know how long. All of my senses are on alert. I've never been so aware of everything around me: every smell, every noise, every sight. The air filling my lungs. The man filling my thoughts.

Minutes later, the bike begins to slow. I hear and feel the gears as Rourke downshifts. Up ahead and to the left, there's a low, long building with a sign I can't read and a large parking lot out front. This must be where we're going.

An unexpected knot of disappointment forms in my stomach that the ride is already over.

Rourke pulls into the lot stops the bike, and cuts the engine. He turns his head, which I take as the sign that I'm supposed to get off first. I let go of him and pull my leg over the seat, awkwardly. I fumble with getting the helmet off, and when I've finally pulled it over my head, I look up to see Rourke grinning at me.

"That didn't take long."

"What didn't?"

He chuckles. "You were hanging onto me tighter than a boa constrictor when we started out. You loosened up pretty quick."

"It was... fun," I admit, letting myself smile back. "When it stopped being so terrifying." I look at the building in front of us. "Where are we?"

"Shooter's," he says simply. "You ever heard of it?"

I shake my head. "Never."

"Best burger you'll ever have. Guaranteed."

I laugh. "I guess that's what I'm getting, then."

"Damn straight you are."

Inside, the atmosphere is raucous, with classic rock booming through the speakers and bartenders pouring beers as fast as they can. Waitresses weave through the crowd delivering plates of food and platters of drinks. Shouts of laughter rise and fall. Over to the side, the clack of pool tables beats a steady rhythm.

"Come on, let's get something to drink," he says. "What'll you have?"

"Just beer is fine."

I follow him to the bar and let him push through to order. A few seconds later he turns back around with glasses of foamy amber liquid, and hands one to me.

"Cheers," I call above the din. "To Mickey. May he be having a miserable time right now."

Rourke bursts into loud laughter. "Now that I can drink to."

As we raise our glasses to drink, I feel Rourke's eyes on me. I find myself wondering what he sees. What he thinks of me. An uptight social worker? A hoity-toity transplant from Louisville with no social life? Something else?

I find that I care about his opinion, very much. A lot more than I want to.

"So," I pipe up, to break the silence. "This is Shooter's. You come here often?"

He shrugs. "Often enough. It's a good ride from Ironwood on

a nice day. And like I said, their burgers can't be beat." His eyes move to a spot in the corner. "Hey. There's Mal and Cyndi."

I turn to look. Over playing darts is one of the Lords I saw at the hospital visiting Bear. With him is a pretty, statuesque blonde who's dressed to the nines, in black leather and lace and thigh-high platform boots. If she rode here on the back of the biker's Harley, I don't know how the heck she did it.

"Let's go on over and say hi," Rourke says, grabbing my hand. He leads me toward them, and I'm so stunned by the contact of his skin that I can barely think as he guides me through the crowds of people. Mal sees us and leans over to say something to the woman. She turns, and when she notices Rourke she breaks into a wide, lipsticked smile and lifts a red-nailed hand in an excited wave.

"Hey, Rourke!" she cries, doing a happy little jump in her heels as we get close. Her eyes move to me, and register just a second's worth of surprise. "Hi!" she says. "I'm Cyndi!"

I'm not sure whether her confusion is because I don't look like Rourke's type, or because she expected to see someone else with him. With an unpleasant jolt, it occurs to me for the first time that he might have a girlfriend. *Or girlfriends, most likely.*

The thought makes my stomach hurt a little. How has it never occurred to me that women are probably all over Rourke? He's definitely one of the most attractive men I've ever seen. And without a doubt, the sexiest. He has this way of holding himself, this way of moving that's both graceful and powerful. It's hard not to stare at him, and I imagine other women would feel the same. I mean, even the nurses at the hospital follow him with their eyes as he moves down the hall.

"You have the most gorgeous hair," Cyndi enthuses. She reaches up to touch the end of my ponytail, which has fallen over my shoulder, but then drops her hand. "Sorry," she laughs. "I'm a hairdresser. It's second nature to me to touch people's hair."

"That's okay," I say automatically.

"Your ends could use a little trim, though," she murmurs, cocking her head. "No offense. I work at Curl up and Dye. You should come by sometime. I'll give you the friends and family discount!"

"Didn't know you had a hot date, Rourke," the biker named Mal jokes. "How you doin', Miss Laney? How'd this degenerate get you to come out with him?"

I open my mouth to reply, but Rourke cuts him off. "None of your fuckin' business, bright boy," he snarls, but Mal just laughs.

"Hey, you wanna play a couple rounds of darts with us?" Cyndi asks. "I don't like playing with Mal because he always smokes me. But maybe with teams we'd be better matched."

"I, uh, don't know how to play darts," I stammer.

Rourke smirks. "No worries. I could beat Mal blindfolded."

"That right, fucker?" Mal retorts.

"I'm about to show you that's right," Rourke shoots back.

It turns out, Rourke is as good as his word. After they explain to me what the different rings on the board mean, we play two rounds of a game they call 301. I have a hard time following the rules, and I'm not much help. It's a victory for me that I can even get the darts on the board at all. But in the end, Rourke and I win both games — or rather, Rourke wins. Mal, pretending to be more pissed than he is, buys us a couple of rounds of shots at the bar as congratulations.

By the time Mal and Cyndi say they're going to take off, I'm feeling fuzzy and loose. As nervous as I was to come here, it turns out I'm having a great time — thank God for alcohol as a social lubricant. Cyndi gives me a big, perfumy hug, and the two of them take off, leaving us sitting on our stools at the bar.

We each order a burger and fries from the bartender. Mine turns out to be just as delicious as Rourke told me it would be.

"That was fun, playing darts with your friends," I grin at Rourke. "Even though I seriously suck at that game."

"You're a beginner. You'll get better. You just need practice."

"This is the most fun I've had in forever, actually," I admit, sliding a fry through my ketchup. "I feel so *normal* right now."

Rourke's amused. "Usually you feel abnormal?"

"You know what I mean. Just a normal, free, happy person. Not Laney the hospital social worker. Not Delaney the senator's daughter."

"Whoa," Rourke says, frowning. "Your dad's a senator?"

Crap, I forgot I never actually told him that. "Oh. Yeah. Senator Rodney Hart, from the great state of Kentucky."

Rourke lets out a high whistle. "You told me your family was a big deal. You didn't tell me they were that big."

I snort. "Yeah. Big freaking deal. Big enough to believe they're better than other people." Blowing out a breath, I hear myself continue, like I'm not even in control of my tongue anymore. "That world has always felt so uncomfortable to me, you know? It's sort of a relief to have moved away from Louisville. Here in Ironwood, nobody knows I'm a senator's daughter. Well, no one but you, that is."

Rourke pretends to lock his lips and throw away the key. "Your secret's safe with me."

"My parents think I'm crazy, living all the way out here. But if I was back in Louisville, I'd probably have been railroaded into getting married to some rich, prominent guy. Like my little sister." I stare at Rourke. "She's marrying a carbon copy of my dad. I'm really afraid she's going to end up like my mom. Basically a prisoner in her marriage. Unable to stand up for herself. No identity except as the wife of someone important."

Rourke's eyes don't leave mine. "Is it really that bad?"

I nod. "Pretty bad. Sometimes I think the only difference between my parents, and Bethany and Mickey, is money. Well, and that Bethany at least had the courage to kick Mickey out once."

"Everybody needs some help sometimes," Rourke responds. "Maybe your mom just needs some help."

"She won't get any," I say gloomily. "She's got too much at stake. Her money. Her life. Her reputation. Mom tries as hard as she can to believe everything is normal. Fine, even." My voice quavers a little. "She'd rather live like this than risk the fear of the unknown."

Shit. I just went from having the time of my life to dragging the whole mood down. "I'm sorry," I laugh, shaking my head against the tears that threaten to come. "I didn't mean to be such a downer."

"It's okay." Rourke's words come out low, even gentle. He's silent for a moment, and then starts talking.

"I have a little sister, too. Regan," he tells me. "Like I told you before. We grew up with an abusive dad. My mom got pregnant with me when they were still in high school. She dropped out before graduation, and got married to him because her family wouldn't help her. Once I was born, she didn't have any money to leave. My sister was born four years later."

I sit silently, trying to digest that Rourke Powers is actually opening up to me about his childhood. He raises his glass and takes a long drink, then continues.

"My mom died from complications from pneumonia when I was nine and Regan was five. By that time, my dad was a full-on drunk." Rourke's expression turns sour. "He didn't much like us kids when Mom was alive, and after she died, he was pissed as hell about having to be a single father. He went back and forth between basically ignoring us and beating the hell out of us."

Rourke trails off, lost in his thoughts for a moment. I'm afraid he'll stop talking if I ask any questions, so I just sit and wait.

"When I was old enough and strong enough, one day I guess I'd just had enough. That weekend, he got drunker than usual and came after me. I kicked his ass and moved out." He raises his glass to his lips, draining it. "I was sixteen. My sister was only twelve, but I couldn't leave her there. I got a job at a garage, after school and on weekends. The place was owned by the dad of a buddy of mine, who knew who and what my father was. I convinced him to let me live in an old RV parked in the back lot of the place.

"I went and got my sister out of the house, and she lived with me in the trailer until I could get us an apartment. I knew my dad would never come looking for us, so I figured we were safe. As long as Child Protective Services never found out."

Rourke's last words are spoken with a sharp, angry edge. Something clicks in my mind.

"But they did," I say softly.

He nods, and shoves his glass away, motioning to the bartender for another.

"Someone at Regan's school figured it out. The social workers came to get us both." Rourke's jaw works as he stares straight ahead. "They couldn't place us both in the same foster home, so they separated us. I spent the next couple years barely seeing her. Hardly even knowing where she was. I figured, once I was eighteen, I'd be able to get her out." His lip curls. "But they said I wasn't an appropriate guardian, or some shit like that."

"God. I'm so sorry, Rourke." I'm starting to understand why he was so hostile to me at first. How could he possibly have a good opinion of social workers, given his own experience?

Rourke blows out a breath. "I've been pissed about it for a long time. But hell, CPS probably thought they were doin' the right thing. Tryin' to find the best solution to a shitty situation."

"Where's your sister now?" I ask, almost afraid of the answer. But to my surprise, Rourke's expression softens.

"She's in college. Senior year. Wants to go to law school, if you can believe that shit." He smiles. "It's takin' her a while, because we're payin' it together, as she goes along."

My chest grows tight. The pride he feels in his sister is obvious. "She's lucky to have a brother like you," I say.

"She deserves all the help I can give her." He turns to me. "She's smart. Like you. You'd like her."

I'm suddenly speechless. A compliment from Rourke seems like rare currency. I don't know how to respond, without showing how moved I am that he thinks anything good of me at all.

"Come on," Rourke murmurs abruptly. He stands up from his stool and takes my arm. "Let's get you back to Ironwood while you're still sober enough not to fall off the bike."

"I'm not drunk at all!" I protest.

He leans in and chuckles low in his throat, the sound sending a burst of tiny explosions of heat through my body. His eyes... *God, his eyes. I could drown in them.* They set me on fire. Flashing gray and black in the low light of the bar, like the Devil himself is looking at me.

"Okay, you got me," he rasps against my ear. "This bar's gettin' a little too crowded for my taste. I want to get you back to Ironwood, and have you all to myself."

18

ROURKE

ood God. There's just something about a girl in a simple white T-shirt and a pair of worn-ass jeans that hug her hips like a lover.

Watching Laney wiggle her ass while she concentrated on aiming those darts was an exercise in torture. I don't think she has any idea how fuckin' good she looks — or that practically every man in Shooter's was staring at her while she took her shots. Hell, even Mal wasn't makin' any secret of it — which earned him more than one dirty look from Cyndi.

I sure as hell liked watching her loosen up at the bar, too. Shit, she's a senator's daughter. No wonder I thought she was a stuck-up bitch when I met her. At least she came by it honestly. I'm still surprised she opened up to me about her family as much as she did tonight. Probably the booze talking, I know. But still, something about the way she looked as she talked about her mom and her sister felt like it's not a story she tells to very many people.

Maybe that's why I found myself talking about my own past. About my piece of shit father, and about Regan.

I wasn't kidding when I told Laney I thought they'd like each other. They're both smart, and fiery, and determined. They're both the type to give any man a hell of a run for his money.

Lord knows Laney's had me going around in circles practically since I met her. Tellin' myself she was a stuck-up bitch I couldn't stand. But even so, somehow I just couldn't fuckin' stay away from her. Couldn't stop myself from thinking about her. Couldn't help wanting to know more about her.

Turns out I've been lying to myself the whole time.

Laney Hart's got herself under my skin.

Deep.

LANEY'S a lot more comfortable on the bike as we ride back to Ironwood. And a lot more friendly, too. She snuggles up against my back, tits pressing against me, and I swear to fuckin' God it's all I can do not to just pull over to the side of the road and take her right there, gawkers be damned.

By the time we get back into town, my cock is aching from being so close to her.

And from the way she's been wriggling against the seat and breathing fast and shallow against my back, I'm guessin' she's pretty hot and bothered herself.

I pull up in front of her place and turn off the engine. As I wait for her to get off the bike, the feel of her hands as they skim low across my stomach almost makes me groan. My cock jumps, so hard and aching that slinging my own leg over the seat is painful. Wordlessly, I walk her up to her front door. I wait for her to unlock and open it, and when she turns to look up at me, her eyes are wide and dark.

Her lips part, trembling a little. "Come in," she whispers.

It's not a question.

She moves inside the doorway, and I'm behind her in a second. The door is barely closed before my mouth is on hers, tasting her, stealing her breath. The same moan she let out the first time I kissed her rips from her throat. I know without even checking she's wet for me. We've been dancing around each other for so long now, our bodies are practically screaming for what we've been denying them. This is happening, and it's happening right now, and it's not up for debate.

My cock swells so large it's painful as my hand reaches up to find the tie that's got her hair up in that ponytail. I loosen it, and the thick locks fall, brushing against my skin. My fingers bury themselves in her hair, pulling her closer so I can kiss her deeper. Laney's hands come up to clutch my shoulders, holding on to me tight, like I'm the only thing keeping her upright. My other arm goes around her waist, sliding down to her ass as I press my throbbing shaft against her core.

She *whimpers*.

Jesus fuck.

Blood thunders in my head as I push her against the wall.

"Do you know how wild you've been driving me, Laney the social worker?" I tell her, my voice thick. "I've played this scene over in my mind a thousand times."

Laney looks up at me, her eyelids fluttering half closed over those green eyes flecked with amber. Her face is tilted up to me, lips swollen and plump already. Ready for me.

"You're not the only one," she whispers.

"Jesus," I hiss, and bend to her again.

Her arms wind around my neck as I drink her in, and it almost undoes me, the way she starts to grind against me like a wild thing. This is a Laney I've never seen before — unafraid, uninhibited, untamed. She kisses me back like I'm water, like I'm air, like I'm her lifeline. Laney's body has taken control; gone is the buttoned up social worker. Gone is the fiery, dark-haired vixen with the tart tongue who has a retort to every word I say. In their place is a girl who needs release — who's giving herself to me and no one else, right here, right now.

My hand slips between us. Somehow I make my brain work

well enough to unzip my jeans, then to slide hers down too. She steps out of them and I grab her ass and lift her onto me, wrapping her legs around my waist. Her whimper turns to a low, needy moan, and I can tell she's already close to coming. There's no way in hell either of us is going to last very long, so I abandon all thoughts of drawing this out. *That will come later. There'll be time for everything else later.* It barely registers that I've never looked forward to the second time with any woman before. And sure as hell not before I've even had her the first time. But there's no fucking way I'll have enough of Laney Hart after just once.

As she writhes against, me, I let out a low groan and move my lips from her mouth to her neck. "Jesus Christ, you feel good, Laney," I growl. "You're gonna be the death of me."

In response, she swivels her hips, all instinct and animal need. "Rourke..." she gasps. "Oh, God, that feels good. Please... more."

Bracing her against the wall, I slide my fingers between us, grazing them against the soaking fabric of her panties. Her sharp intake of breath makes my cock swell as I realize how close she is. She clings tighter to me and moans again, shuddering slightly at the contact of my finger as I slip it under the fabric. Then it's my turn to moan. She's so wet. Wet for me. Wet for this.

Then, my other hand cupping her ass, I slide the pulsing head of my cock against the slick skin of her pussy.

It's only for a second or two, but suddenly Laney goes completely rigid. Then, a moment later, she shatters, shuddering against me as her orgasm tears through her. Knowing I'm only seconds behind her, I shove my hips forward and drive myself inside her. Laney gasps and throws her head back, breathing ragged. She's so goddamn tight, her walls pulsing around me, and the blood gets louder in my head, my vision tunneling until all I see is her face, mouth half-open in ecstasy, every cell of her body mine right now, all mine...

I piston in and out of her one final time, and then everything explodes around me as I empty myself deep inside her, holding her close as the world blurs completely, then slowly — so slowly — comes back into focus.

She's still in my arms, her legs wrapped around mine as I carry her through the house, lit only by the dim light of the street lamp outside and a small night light in the hall.

"Last door on the left," she murmurs against my chest, already starting to sound sleepy.

And then, it hits me.

A wave of anger at myself washes over me as I realize how badly I just fucked up. I've just done something I've *never* allowed myself to do before.

"Shit," I murmur against her hair.

"What?" she asks, alarmed. She lifts her head from my chest and looks into my eyes.

"Fuck, Laney, I forgot to use a condom. I'm sorry. Jesus, I swear it didn't even cross my mind."

For a split-second I'm sure she doesn't believe me, and the thought makes me feel sick inside. Then her eyes soften.

"I'm on the shot," she tells me, with a slight shake of her head. "And I haven't had sex in... well..." She ducks her head. "Awhile, let's just say."

We're in her bedroom now. I lean down and sit down on the bed, with her still wrapped around me.

"I swear to God I'm clean," I promise her. "I don't fuck without wrapping up Vlad the Impaler first. Ever."

She blinks in surprise, and then starts to giggle helplessly.

"Seriously?" she gasps in between giggles. "You call your dick Vlad the Impaler?"

"No," I admit. "I just said that to make you laugh."

I'M NOT EVEN CLOSE to having enough of Laney. The second time I take her is slower, though not much gentler. And when she calls out my name as she shudders underneath me, I feel like the king of the goddamn world.

Afterwards, she falls asleep in my arms.

And for the first time in my life, it never even occurs to me to leave.

I barely sleep, though. Instead, I just lie there staring up at the ceiling, listening to her breathe.

Just as her bedroom starts to lighten with the first pinks of the morning sun, I slip out of bed and pull on my clothes. I need to go home and grab a shower, then get to the clubhouse in time for the run to meet with Chaco Dos Santos.

I'm quiet as I move around the room. In the half-light, I watch Laney for a few seconds as she sleeps. Her hair is strewn around her face on the pillow. The sheets are down just far enough for me to catch the swell of her breasts.

As I remember her soft cries last night when she came around my cock, I have to talk myself out of climbing back into the bed with her. I surprise myself by being damn disappointed I'm not gonna be here when she wakes up.

I leave her house, careful to lock the door behind me. To keep her safe, until I can see her again.

Which is gonna be just as soon as I get back to Ironwood after the run.

I put the bike into neutral, and roll it down her driveway, making sure I'm away from the house before I fire it up. Because I don't want to wake her. I want to drive away with the picture of her in my mind, lying there on the bed, face soft in sleep, hair streaming around her.

What the fuck is wrong with me?

I've never spent the night with a woman. That's by choice. I'm not a guy who does long-term. Hell, I'm not even a guy who does short-term. I don't need the complication of having any woman think fucking is more than just fucking.

But God help me, I think this time maybe it is.

I think I'm falling for Laney Hart.

19

ROURKE

T he road to Louisville is state highways for about half the time, and interstate for the other half. We make it to the outskirts of the city in about three hours.

We're meeting Chaco Dos Santos in an industrial suburb on the north side. The meetup spot is a shitty old unassuming Mexican restaurant, where we've met Chaco and his men before. Just like last time, the place is deserted when we get there, with not a customer in sight. And of course, that's by design. It's a mystery as to why anyone ever opened up a restaurant here in the first place. It's surrounded by warehouses, lumber and building wholesalers, and even a chemical factory, but since it's Sunday most of these businesses are shuttered for the weekend. But for the purpose of having a meeting undisturbed, it's perfect.

When we go inside, a short old Mexican guy sits at the till, but otherwise the place is deserted. The stale stench of Mexican cooking assaults my nostrils. I'm not a fan of Mexican food in the first place, but it smells like no one's actually ordered food here in months.

Axel, me, Dante, and Mal walk through restaurant, ignoring the old guy. Chaco's in the same back room he's met us in before.

He's there with four other guys, two of whom I recognize from the last time. They flank him, standing like silent sentinels.

Unlike last time we were here, Chaco doesn't ask us to remove our pieces. He comes around the long table in the center of the room, and Axel and Chaco clap each other on the back, a sign of trust. He nods to me, a sign of respect as Axel's VP, then motions toward the table, indicating we should sit down. Axel shoots a glance at me, and I take a seat to his right. Dante and Mal stay standing, mirroring Chaco's bodyguards.

Last time we met here, Chaco was the one with the upper hand. Our chapter of the Lords of Carnage was taking over part of the transfer route of Chaco's product from northern Kentucky through southern Ohio, as far as the Tanner Springs chapter of the Lords to our north. Chaco wasn't happy with that arrangement. Angel, the prez of the Tanner Springs chapter, sent down one of his men, Hale, to smooth over the transition. Chaco accepted it, but he had his doubts about working with Axel and the Ironwood club, instead of directly with Angel.

Hale, speaking for Angel, gave him his assurance that the transition would be smooth and that our club was up to the task. We knew that if there were any problems with the shipment transfers on our end, the cartel would look at doing business with another MC or some other syndicate.

Which would mean moving to take us out, to free up our territory for someone else.

This time, the tables have turned. Now it's Ironwood that needs assurance from Chaco that they're gonna have the product we need, when we need it. And even before he starts talking, it's clear that Chaco is not happy to be seen in this position of weakness. Everything about this guy telegraphs how proud he is — from his two-thousand dollar suits to the straight, formal way he carries himself. Everything about his bearing says he expects to be treated like a king, and his men comply.

"So, Chaco, what's the deal?" Axel asks, cutting to the chase right away. "Your latest shipment was supposed to get to us tomorrow. I'm guessing this meeting ain't because you were graciously wanting to give it to us a day early."

"No. Clearly not." Chaco's voice is low and steely. He is angry. But he knows he can't afford to let the anger loose.

"I talked to Angel yesterday," Axel continues. "Let him know about this meeting. He's not happy. You know we're looking to expand our distribution up north. This larger shipment was supposed to be the first step in that."

I step in. "Last time we were here, you told us the Dos Santos cartel had entered into a relationship with Los Caballeros. You said your two cartels together had more than enough strength to push back Sinaloa from your territory."

"The product is here," Chaco grits out. "The problem is not there. The problem is... a matter of accessing the shipment."

"What do you mean?" Axel retorts.

"As I told you, our problem is we're not able to get close to it. There are fucking cops all over us. They don't know the exact location where we're holding the product, but they clearly know the general area. They swarm every time my men try to get near." His face contorts.

"They ain't geniuses," Mal jokes. "If they were smart, they'd be better at hanging back and catchin' you in the act, instead of showing themselves. Fuck, I thought Louisville cops wouldn't be such dumbasses."

Chaco shoots a glare at Mal, but says nothing.

"Who tipped them off?" Axel sounds calm, but I know better. He's fucking furious.

"Unsure."

"What about your buddies Los Caballeros?"

Chaco says nothing. But the way his eyes narrow tell me Axel may have hit a nerve.

It makes sense. Los Caballeros are supposed to be their allies — the two groups a united front to keep their territory away from

Sinaloa. But allies are only as good as the deal you've made with them.

And if an ally sees a better deal somewhere else...

Then the line between ally and enemy gets real thin, real fast.

"So. What are our options here?" Axel demands. "We need this shipment, Chaco. You don't hold up your end of the deal, we get screwed on our end."

Tension in the room heightens. From an outlaws' gentleman's agreement, we're going down the road to something totally different. The Lords of Carnage can't afford to let this shit slide. Our own dominance, the strength of our club, depends on other clubs knowing we cannot be fucked with.

"We have another contact." Chaco's words are clipped. "We need an extra day. But we will get you the entire volume of the shipment. Our drop point will change, but you can be assured —"

A muffled shout outside interrupts his words.

Then, a deafening blast.

Gunfire.

"Get down!" Axel shouts. I dive for the ground, just as the thin wood of the closed door splinters like toothpicks. Jesus. I barely have time to reach for my piece when another volley of gunfire blasts through it. Rolling off to one side, I pull it out and grab the base of a small table, pulling it down until it crashes to the floor. I push it in front of me to serve as a shield. It's not enough to cover me, but it's all I got.

Raising my gun, I fire off a round at the door. I've only got one goddamn magazine, so I have to make each bullet count. By now, my ears are roaring with all the blasts around me. I hear a couple of cries through the wall of sound, but I can't tell who's being hit, or where. A couple of Chaco's men had ARs, but shit's happening so fast I don't know where they are now. Across the room Mal is aiming toward the door, rapid flashes of fire from his gun showing me his shots.

We're sitting fucking ducks in this room, unless we can blast ourselves out.

My mind goes into survival mode as I pull myself into a crouch and prepare to move. Just before I spring, my eyes fall on a wad of gum smushed under the table I'm hiding behind.

For some reason, that makes me laugh out fucking loud.

Reaching behind me, I grab the metal leg of a chair in my left hand, and stand up. I pull myself against the wall, just on one side of the doorway, and try to trust that Dos Santos' men and my brothers' aims are good enough not to hit me instead of whoever's on the other side.

When the first asshole manages to make it through and into the room, I bring the chair up and around, smashing him in the skull before he knows what's happening. He falls to the floor and the guy behind him stumbles over him. His piece flies out of his hands, ricocheting off my boot. I use two of my bullets to take them both out, then grab the dropped gun, a Glock 19 with an extended mag. *Good fuckin' deal.*

Mal and Axel are up now, too, guns drawn. Chaco's two bodyguards appear behind us, then move ahead, unleashing a spray of fire. We move in and prepare to follow their lead.

But then, a loud shot behind me stops me in my tracks.

I pivot quickly, just in time to see Chaco fall to the ground. One of the two men next to him holds a gun at his side, finger still on the trigger.

Holy fuck. At least one of Chaco's men has turned.

I lift my eyes just in time to see the other guy raise his piece toward us. Instinctively, I throw the the chair I'm still holding toward him, launching it through the air without time to aim. It's enough to make him duck, which gives me a couple seconds to launch myself at him. I barrel forward, and just before I connect, a dull wave of pressure on my upper thigh pushes me a little to one side.

Fuck, I think as I take the fucker down. *I'm shot.*

There's no time to think about it. I hear more gunfire and shouting, but I wrestle the asshole I've got to the ground and grab his wrist. As he tries to kick me off of him, I bring his hand down repeatedly against the floor until his grip loosens on the gun. When he's let go of it, I pull back and fire a hard right to his face with the butt of my gun. It gets him in the jaw, sending him reeling. A second punch to his temple takes him out.

I scramble up, but my left leg starts to crumple under me. I reach back to my upper thigh and feel around. Wet. The fabric of my jeans is ripped just below my ass cheek.

I roll onto my side, angling myself to face the door, and get ready to fire. Next to me, Chaco's breathing is labored, blood blooming a stain across his shirt. Ten feet away, Dante's got the other traitor on the ground. I start to raise my gun, hoping to get a clear shot. But before I can, there's a loud crack. The guy Dante's wrestling stiffens, then his body falls slack.

Have a good trip to hell, motherfucker.

It's only in the seconds after Dante shoots the second traitor that I realize the gunfire outside has stopped. I haul myself to my feet, favoring my left leg. The wound is burning now, and my ass is starting to go numb, but the leg itself is at least supporting my weight.

Dante calls over to me. "You okay?"

"Yeah." I lift my chin toward Chaco. "We gotta get him some help."

I raise my gun and consider shooting the asshole I knocked out, but figure we're better off getting as much information out of him as we can before ending him. Limping, I go to the doorway and yell out for Axel. His voice comes back a second later.

"We're clear," he shouts.

"We need some help here!" I call back. "Chaco's down!"

FIFTEEN MINUTES LATER, the Dos Santos cartel has hauled off the traitor I punched out — no doubt taking him somewhere to extract as much intel out of him as possible before shooting the motherfucker. A doc has arrived — a large, rotund man who takes one look at Chaco and shoos us all out of the back room except for a few of Chaco's men. By now my ass is burning from the gunshot wound, but I've figured out it's just a surface wound and fairly clean, so it ain't as bad as it could have been. Axel sends Mal in to the doc to grab some bandages and a shot of something to numb the pain.

"You good to ride, brother?" Axel asks me as Mal comes back.

"Yeah," I grit out. "I'll be okay. Just need to patch this shit up."

"Well, I ain't doin' it," Mal jokes. "I ain't gettin' any closer to your hairy ass than I have to."

"You dream of that shit," I fire back. "Just give me the goddamn stuff and let me do it myself. It'll be good enough until I can have Reno take a look at it when I get back." Reno's our resident medical guy. He was a medic in Afghanistan, and the fucker knows his shit.

I'm getting ready to hobble off to the bathroom to tape myself up when something occurs to me.

"Hey, where's the old guy?" I frown, nodding toward the front register where the owner was sitting earlier.

Dante's lip curls. "The guards Chaco had posted outside the restaurant caught him runnin' away before the attack."

"Jesus." I shake my head. "He was in on it, too. Goddamnit."

"Yeah," Axel agrees, disgusted. "Safe to say, that's the last time he'll betray the Dos Santos cartel. Or anyone else."

20

LANEY

Rourke is gone when I wake up the next morning.

At first, I think maybe he's just gotten up before me. But as I lie in bed, the silence in the house tells me he's not here. And when I finally raise myself up to a sitting position, I see his clothes are gone as well. The imprint of his head on the pillow next to me is the only indicator that last night wasn't a dream.

Well, that, and the pleasant soreness between my legs.

He didn't leave a note or anything. Nothing to say when he left, or why. As I haul myself up out of bed and start my morning routine, I try to tell myself that's a good thing. I mean, what was I expecting him to say? *Laney, you're the love of my life, I'll count the seconds until I can come back and sweep you away to our new life together?*

I mean, that's just silly.

Would I even want him to say that?

What *do* I want, anyway?

It's safe to say my feelings about last night are confused. On the one hand, I have to be honest — sex with Rourke Powers was the best I've ever had. Even the frenetic first time, pushed up against the wall of my living room, ranks among the all-time best orgasms I've ever had. And then, the second time...

My face flames at the memory. Oh my God. I had no idea it could feel like that. Hard, and soft, and frantic, and slow. I always laughed at that ridiculous expression, *The earth moved*. But honestly?

After last night, I sort of get it.

I wonder over my morning cup of coffee whether I'm even going to see Rourke again. The thought that I might not sends a pang of alarm through my chest. But realistically, there's no reason I would. Is there? I mean, we aren't dating. We aren't even exactly friends. More like two opponents who united around a common enemy. Last night was just a victory celebration. A victory celebration with mind-blowing sex, yes. But I'm pretty sure that's all it was.

And that's probably all it should be. I'm hardly Rourke's type. Granted, I don't know what his type is, exactly, but I'm guessing it's more like Cyndi. Leggy. Busty. Looking like she'd be perfect as a model at a Harley show.

I'm just Laney the social worker. As he makes sure not to let me forget.

On the ride to work, I'm still trying to talk myself into thinking it's okay if last night was the end of Rourke and me. But the fact that I have literally been thinking about him for every single second since I woke up tells me it's going to be tough to shove him out of my head.

It's been a long time since I pined after a boy — since my freshman year of college to be exact, when my secret crush Jim Iocca got drunk at an off-campus party and kissed me, then proceeded to ignore me for the entire rest of the year. I was a ridiculous mess about it, following him around and just "happening" to show up at places I knew he would be.

I refuse to be such a weirdo about this thing with Rourke.

You're a strong, mature woman, I chide myself. *Besides, we're from two different worlds. You're not his type, and he's not yours.*

The thing is, though... Rourke? He may be a biker. And he may have scared the crap out of me the first time I met him. The world may look at him like he's a lowlife, or a criminal.

But he's a better man than most men I know. Including my senator father.

If my parents met Rourke, they would be horrified by him. They would lose their minds if he and I got together.

But Rourke Powers is worth ten of Rodney Hart.

Whatever happened between us last night may already be over. I don't know.

But if I'm honest with myself, I don't want it to be.

"YOU'RE IN A GOOD MOOD," Katie says, furrowing her brow.

"Am I?" I reply breezily.

"Yes." She cocks her head at me. "You're less uptight than usual."

"Um... thanks?" I guess I should be offended, but I just laugh.

"You know what I mean. You're..." Katie waves her hand around at me. "You're not walking like you walk. All buttoned up and professional. You..." Her eyes widen. "You look like you got laid."

I laugh again, but this time it sounds forced, even to me.

"Oh, come on," I scoff. "That's ridiculous. People don't actually look different after they've had sex. That's just a thing people say in the movies."

"Uh, I guess it's *not* just a thing they say in the movies," she smirks, crossing her arms and giving me a knowing stare. "Because *you* are blushing! So don't give me that B.S. Girl, you. Got. Laid."

Shit. I can keep lying, but Katie's on this like a dog with a bone now. I know her well enough to know she's not going to let up. So I pull in a deep breath and roll my eyes.

"People have sex, Katie," I sigh, trying for a *stop-making-such-a-big-deal-out-of-nothing* tone. "Though I'm not exactly happy to learn that I walk like I have a stick up my butt."

"So, who is it?" Katie presses, ignoring me. "You didn't mention meeting anyone or going on any dates recently. And, you don't have a social life. So where did you find this guy?"

"Okay, seriously? Is this Insult Laney Day?"

"Oh, come on," she snorts. "You're the first to admit your social calendar is basically nonexistent. The only place you even come into contact with people of the opposite sex is here at the hospital. And..." Katie trails off, and then her eyes practically pop out of her head.

"It's the biker, isn't it?" she breathes.

"Katie..."

"It *is*! Oh, my God!" She stares at me in shock. And not the good kind of shock. "Oh my *God*, Laney!" she repeats, her voice rising. "I mean, I know he kissed you in the coffee shop, but I figured you'd come to your senses before..." She shakes her head. "Good lord, are you crazy?"

"It was just one date," I protest.

"'*Date*'!" she snorts. "For God's sake, Laney, you don't know a single thing about him!" Katie flings her hands in the air. "What is *wrong* with you? God, you basically live like a nun for as long as I've known you, and now this? Talk about going to extremes! How can you have just done everything you can to get Mickey away from Bethany and Paisley, and then fall into the arms of a man who's probably ten times more dangerous?"

My cheeks flame with indignation. "Katie, that is absolutely ridiculous."

"How do you know?" She reaches up and points a finger at my face. "How do you know? You think this biker thing is just an act? You think he collects stamps for a hobby, or something?"

"I just do," I shoot back, sounding lame even to myself. But it's true. Somehow I *do*.

I have no doubt he could be dangerous as hell, to the person who got on his wrong side.

But I also know deep down, there's a kindness to him. And he always holds the door open for me. And he's told me about how hard he tried to protect his sister from their father.

I don't feel comfortable sharing any of that with Katie, though. It would feel like I was betraying a confidence, somehow.

"He's not..." I cast about for the right words. "He's not like that. Come on, Katie, think! Rourke is the whole reason his club stood guard outside Paisley's room to keep her safe. What kind of person would do that, if he didn't have a heart?"

"Holy moly," she breathes. "You've got it bad." She starts to shake her head in disbelief, but then stops to stare at me, eyes wide. "Wait — is this why you roped me into your crazy plan?" Katie cries, then claps a hand over her face. She continues, her tone lower but clearly furious. "Is *this* why you wanted me to help you with 'the thing'?" she challenges me. "Because you wanted to impress *Rourke*?"

"No! God!" I grab her arm and pull her into a side hallway. "You know why I did that! I wanted to help Paisley and Bethany! And it worked, didn't it? Like a charm!"

"For you, maybe!" she retorts. "But guess who wants to see me in his office later, to 'ask me some questions' about how Mickey managed to corner me in the med closet?"

My eyes widen.

"Shit," I hiss. *Blake.*

Somehow, it hadn't occurred to me that he'd feel the need to investigate this. Not since Mickey got caught, and no drugs actually ended up getting stolen.

"Maybe it's just a formality?" I ask, feeling sick.

Katie shakes her head, clearly worried. "I don't know. But he made it clear he wanted to, and I quote, 'get to the bottom of this.'" She puts air quotes around the phrase.

"What bottom?" I protest. "It's over! It's not your fault Mickey followed you and tried to rob the hospital?"

"Isn't it?" Katie asks, shooting me a pointed look.

Oh, God. "No. It's not," I say softly. "It's mine."

"Laney, what if he isn't satisfied by my answers?" Katie asks, her voice starting to rise again. "What if he decides he needs to make an example of me, for the rest of the hospital?"

"He wouldn't fire you, Katie," I insist. "You're one of the best nurses Morningside has. He'd be a fool to lose you."

"You know he does weird stuff all the time, Laney!" She grips my arm, her features strained like she's trying not to panic. "He's not rational when he feels like he's got something to prove! I can't lose my job!"

"I know," I murmur. Katie's a single mom to a little boy with special needs and a raft of health problems. She need the benefits, and the money. She has no safety net. My stomach churns at the possibility that she could be fired.

"I never should have gone along with your ridiculous plan," Katie mutters, shaking her head. "It was a crazy thing to do, Laney! I should have known better. I should have realized your judgment was clouded because of that biker!"

I open my mouth to shoot back a retort, but then close it again.

Is Katie right that my judgment was clouded because this was Rourke's idea? I didn't think so before. But now, with Katie potentially in trouble, I honestly don't know.

"Katie, listen!" I say, grabbing her hand. "I swear, this will not come down on you. If push comes to shove, tell Blake — I don't know, tell him anything!" I think quickly. "Tell him I was the one who told Mickey he could get drugs by following you into the med closet! If he comes and asks me, I'll admit it. I'll fall on the sword."

She stares at me. "You'd do that for me?"

"Absolutely." I don't even hesitate. "This is completely my fault. Throw me under the bus if you have to. Tell him you had your suspicions, and I admitted it when you confronted me. Make it sound like you were the one who figured it out. Make sure he realizes you're the one bringing him the guilty party, okay? Then when he calls me in, I'll admit everything. The worst you would get is a slap on the wrist."

"But — but then *you'd* lose your job!" she cries. "And you might never be able to work at a hospital again."

"I don't care," I say firmly. "I'd find another job. This is on me, Katie. Like you said, I talked you into this whole thing. If anyone gets punished for it, it should be me."

I spend the next few minutes extracting a promise from Katie that she'll tell Blake I'm the guilty one if she has to. It only partly alleviates how sick I feel that I got her involved in this in the first place.

But at this point, it's all I can do.

Shaken and antsy after my conversation with Katie, I decide to go down to the coffee shop — because of course, pouring caffeine over my already rattled nerves is the mature response to my problem. I'm hoping a fancy coffee with lots of sugar and whipped cream will be just the comfort and distraction I need.

I decide to take the stairs down instead of the elevator, to at least get a little more exercise to offset the decadence. Pushing the fire door open on the first floor, I turn toward the main entrance, and head through it toward the wing with the coffee shop. I'm completely lost in my own thoughts as I order the most decadent coffee drink I can think of, and watch the barista put extra whipped cream on it. My teeth practically hurt just from thinking about all the sugar I'm going to consume, but dammit, I deserve this right now.

After paying for my mocha, I head back down the hallway, on autopilot except for the single sip of creamy goodness I allow myself before I'm back inside my office. The bustle of late after-noon in the front atrium is so familiar to me that I barely pay any attention to the figures milling back and forth.

Which is why I almost don't register the bloodied, limping figure as it comes through the entrance and heads toward me.

When I finally do see who it is, my jaw practically drops to the floor.

"Oh, my God, Rourke!" I gasp. "Holy shit! What in the hell happened to you?"

21

ROURKE

The ride back to Ironwood hurts like a motherfucker, but I'll live.

When we get back to town a couple of hours, I stop off at the clubhouse with the rest of the brothers just long enough to have Reno verify that the bullet I took just grazed my ass.

Then I get back on the bike and head straight for Morningside Hospital.

Turns out, I don't even have to go to Laney's office to find her. I see her almost as soon as I push through the doors. She's walking through the main lobby atrium area, probably on her way to her office, a massive to-go cup from the coffee shop in one hand. I'm just about to call her name when her eyes fall on me.

"Oh, my God, Rourke!" she gasps, almost dropping the cup. She practically runs to me. "Holy shit! What in the hell happened to you?"

"I think that's the first time I've heard you swear," I joke.

"Well, it's warranted." Laney's eyes are wide with shock. "Look at you! What happened?"

The sudden paleness of her skin makes her lips look all the

more pink and pillowy. My cock snaps to attention despite the pain I'm in.

I mean, this gunshot ain't that big a deal — I don't look *that* bad — but it kind of does something to me that she cares.

"Uh, just a little accident," I shrug.

"*Accident?*"

"I got shot. But it's nothing. Just a flesh wound."

"Shot?" she cries. A couple people in the atrium look over. Laney shakes her head and lowers her tone. "What do you mean, shot?" she asks in alarm.

"Like, someone fires a gun, and..."

"Oh, my God, you are *not* going to joke about this, are you?" She looks at me like I'm nuts. "You know what? Forget it. Let's get you over to patient admissions," she murmurs, coming close and putting a hand on my arm. My dick jolts again at the contact with her, but I ignore it.

"What?" I ask, confused, and then start laughing. "Laney, I ain't here to check in."

She blinks. "You have got to be kidding me."

I snort. "Darlin', if I checked into the hospital every time I got a scratch, I'd be in here all the damn time. And believe me, this is just a scratch."

"Good lord," she groans. "I suppose I don't want to know what happened that someone actually shot at you. Though, you are annoying enough that it doesn't take all that much imagination."

I take it as a good sign that she's giving me shit. "Is that any way to talk to the man who helped you get Mickey out of the picture?" I protest.

She stares up at me and cocks her head. "Between Bear getting stabbed and you getting shot, I'm starting to think staying far away from you is a really good idea."

"You serious?"

Laney pulls in a deep breath and sighs it out.

"No," she admits. "So why are you here?"

"Second date."

"Second —!" Laney's eyes get even wider. Then, she bursts out laughing so hard I think she might pee herself.

"What?" I deadpan. "The first date wasn't good?"

"Oh, my God," she gasps, reaching up to wipe at her eyes with her free wrist. "Rourke, I have to hand it to you, I literally never know what is going to come out of your mouth."

"That's good, right?" I say, a corner of my mouth lifting.

She smirks back, pretending to be exasperated. "Well, it's interesting, I'll give you that."

"So, you up for a ride?" I ask, sliding my eyes over her. "I see you're wearing pants today."

She raises her free hand to pinch the bridge of her nose. "I don't know. It's been a long day. I guess so. Are you taking me back to Shooter's?"

"Nope. Somewhere else. Thought you might like to pay Bethany and Paisley a visit."

LANEY'S GOT about an hour left to work, so I hang out in the front atrium for a while, then go outside for a smoke. She comes out right on schedule, pulling her hair into a ponytail as she walks toward me.

"Are you going to bring me back here to the hospital to get my car later?" she asks, accepting the helmet I offer her.

"Will it be okay here overnight, just in case?"

She cocks her head and gives me a knowing smirk. "What are you suggesting?"

I grab her and pull her close. "I'm suggesting I want a replay of last night," I growl against her ear. "That okay with you?"

Her answer comes out breathy. "I suppose I wouldn't mind that," she teases.

This time, when she gets on the back of my bike, she settles right in. Instead of going rigid with fear, Laney nestles against my back and wraps her arms around my torso. After what happened between us last night, the contact of her body against mine makes me hard as hell, and I struggle to keep my focus on the road.

When I pull us up to the clubhouse compound a few minutes later, I feel her body shift as she looks around, taking it all in. It's just after six, and our legit business, Ironwood Car and Truck Repair, is just closing up for the day. In the back lot, a couple of the brothers are taking advantage of the warm evening to break out the grill. The smell of cooking meat wafts our way.

"I thought you said you wanted a replay of last night," Laney says through her helmet once I've killed the engine.

"Like I said, I thought you might like to see Bethany and Paisley first," I answer. "This is our clubhouse."

"Are they here?" she asks as she climbs off, surprised.

I nod. "Yoda brought them here to stay for a bit after Paisley got discharged. Thought they might do better right at first somewhere with people around."

Laney frowns. "Are you sure that's such a good idea?"

"What do you mean?"

"I mean..." she looks at the row of bikes, and nods toward the clubhouse with a frown. "Is this the kind of place a little kid should be?"

"You mean compared to a shitty motel room with memories of her mom's asshole boyfriend?" I smirk. "Come on. Let's go inside, and you can judge for yourself."

I lead her to the front door. Laney steps through, hesitating, like she's not quite sure what to expect. Tonight the clubhouse is less rowdy than usual, since some of the old ladies and their kids are here for the barbecue. I let Laney look around the big main room, watching her as she takes in the bar, the pool tables in the center of the room, and the big pit toward the back with low, comfortable sofas. Paisley and Bethany are over there. They're with Bailey, Gage's old lady, and Bailey's little girl, Addi. Paisley and Addi are sitting on the large shag rug between the couches, playing some board game or other I don't recognize.

Bethany looks up and waves when she sees us, and I lead Laney over.

"Paisley, look who's here!" Bethany says to her daughter.

"Laney!" Paisley cries, flinging herself to her feet. She races over. Laney bends down and gives her a hug.

"How are you doing?" Laney asks."I like your shirt!" Paisley's wearing a blue T-shirt with a unicorn on it. Her hair's pulled up in a matching blue scrunchie thing.

"Addi gave it to me!" she says, turning to Bailey's daughter. Paisley looks proud as hell. I can't tell if it's because of the fancy shirt, or because she's got a new friend. Probably it's both, the poor kid.

Bailey stands up. "Hi, Laney. I'm Bailey. And that little rascal sitting next to Paisley is Addi."

"Hi," Addi grins, looking up from the game.

"We brought some of Addi's clothes that didn't fit her anymore," Bailey continues. "We thought Paisley could use them, and it turns out she's the perfect size for them."

"That's very nice of you," Laney smiles.

"Bailey is with one of the other Lords," I tell Laney. "Gage. He's outside manning the grill."

"Gage and Dante are making hot dogs and hamburgers," Addi tells us. "And steak for the grown-ups."

Laney nods her head. "That sounds really good." She turns to me. "Are we staying for dinner?"

"If you're good with that."

"I am." Her eyes sparkle.

"Good deal. Come on over to the bar. I'll grab us something to drink."

Laney follows me, nodding back toward the other women. "I guess I'll just take a Coke for now," she says.

One of the prospects is behind the counter, and I order a

Coke for Laney and a bottle of beer for me. As he's leaning down to grab our drinks, Bear comes ambling over.

"Well, well, well," he rumbles at Laney. "Thought I'd managed to leave that damn hospital behind." He nods toward the prospect and asks for a shot of whiskey.

For a second I think Laney's going to get offended or upset, but she just laughs. "Don't worry, Bear, I'm off the clock. I'm not here to spy on you or make sure you're taking your meds."

"Thank Christ for that," he mutters.

"Although, I'm not sure you're supposed to be drinking while you're still on your painkillers," she teases.

"This *is* a painkiller," he points out, lifting the shot glass. "Better'n those damn pills."

Laney holds up her hands. "You're an adult. You do what you need to do."

"Damn straight." Bear looks at me. "At least she knows what's what."

"That she does."

Bear raises his shot glass at us and wanders off. Laney watches him go.

"This is... weird," she murmurs.

"What is?"

"I guess I thought your clubhouse would be like this scary, dangerous place." She shakes her head and laughs softly. "Except for the tattoos and the leather, it's all pretty... normal."

I chuckle. "Well, it's not always this tame. But yeah, some of the brothers have families, of course, so their old ladies and kids come around, too. And Paisley... well, for obvious reasons, she's kind of become our mascot for now. Yoda asked our prez, Axel, if he could bring her and Bethany here to make sure they're okay. Just until we know what's happening with Mickey."

"Oh, gosh. Any news on that front?"

"I talked to my cop friend. He says Mickey's gonna have a bail hearing tomorrow."

Laney's brow creases with worry. "Do you think he'll get out?"

"Could be, but I doubt it." I take a long pull of my beer, leaning against the bar. "Bethany told Yoda she ain't gonna post bail for him. Not that she has the money, anyway. So, it depends on whether he can get some other sucker to spring him out."

Laney blows out a breath. "I hope not."

"Don't worry," I reassure her. "Paisley and Bethany are under the club's protection now." I grab my beer and stand. "Look, I'm gonna go outside and make sure Gage and Dante don't burn the meat. Those fuckers don't know shit about grilling. Will you be okay here for a few minutes?"

"Sure." She gives me an easy smile. "I'll go talk to Bethany and Bailey. I wanted to ask Bethany some things anyway."

"Okay," I nod. I pull her in for a kiss that leaves her a little breathless and flushed when I'm done with her. "You make yourself at home. Anyone gives you any trouble, you tell them you're with me. I'll be back in a little bit."

22

LANEY

"Paisley looks more relaxed than I've ever seen her," I say to Bethany.

I watch Rourke's back as he limps away from me, shaking my head. How is that man even standing after getting shot? Much less acting like nothing even happened. I know he said it was just a flesh wound, but still.

What have I gotten myself into with him?

Bethany lets out a happy sigh. "I know," she agrees. "It's so nice to see her just happy and carefree for a change. Addi is being so nice to her!"

"Addi really likes Paisley," Addi's mother, Bailey, says. She's about my height and slightly thinner than I am. Feature-wise, we could almost be sisters. Her dark hair is a shade lighter than mine, her face a little softer. "She took to her right away. I think those two are going to be thick as thieves."

"I guess I never really realized it before," Bethany murmurs. "But I don't think Paisley has very many friends at school." She shakes her head. "And, well, with our situation... It's not like she gets to have a lot of play dates."

Bailey gives her a kind look. "I'm a teacher at Ironwood

Elementary. Addi's a year ahead of Paisley. I get the impression from listening to Paisley that she's had some trouble being bullied?"

Bethany nods.

"Well, Addi's a good friend. Very loyal. She'll watch out for her. I can check and see if they have the same recess. That would be great, for both of them."

"Your daughter seems like such a sweet little girl," I tell Bailey.

"Thank you," she smiles. "I think so." She nods toward the front door. "And she adores Gage."

"Is he her daddy?"

"No. Addi's father and I are divorced." She lowers her voice a notch. "Frankly, Garrett never had much interest in being a father. So it's great for Addi that Gage is so good with her."

We watch in silence on the couch as Paisley and Addi concentrate on their board game. Their young faces are so serious as they play, it's incredibly sweet. I find myself swallowing around a sudden lump in my throat. It's true what I said to Bethany: I've never seen Paisley so relaxed. Her little forehead is free from creases, smooth and untroubled.

Bethany starts to speak, almost as though to herself. "I... I just haven't been able to provide much for her lately, you know? It seems like it takes everything I have in me, just to keep us above water. And now, with these hospital bills..."

Bethany's voice wobbles a little, as though she's trying not to cry. I turn to look at her, and see the worry in her face. Reaching out, I put a hand on top of hers. It's cold.

"Bethany," I say quietly. ""I know you've been going through a rough spot. I know you're worried about money. But I have been able to find you some resources. We can talk about that tomorrow, if you'd like. Can you stop by the hospital sometime? I'll clear my calendar for whenever you're free."

She blinks back tears and nods. "Yes. I can. I'm going to take Paisley back to school tomorrow afternoon. I thought I should start her out on half-days for a day or two, just to make sure she's up for it. I can come by the hospital after I drop her off."

"Good," I say, patting her hand. "So, are you going back to the motel tonight?"

"No-o-o..." Bethany trails off, and her face starts to pink. "We're staying here for the night. Yoda said he'd give us his apartment to stay in."

"His apartment?" I frown.

Bethany points down a long corridor. "This place is bigger than it looks. There's a whole other area back there, with a bunch of separate apartments that the men use."

"So, uh, Bethany," Bailey pipes in, a mischievous look on her pretty face. "What *is* going on with you and Yoda, anyway?"

The pink of Bethany's cheeks turns brighter. "Nothing. At least, not exactly. He's just being nice to me. I mean, he wants something more. And honestly, I think I do, too. But he's giving me space right now."

"So, does that mean things are finished between you and Mickey?" I ask.

"Yes." Bethany's tone turns stronger. "I haven't told him yet, exactly. But it's over. He thought he could come back after he hurt Paisley. And I almost let him." Her jaw juts out a little as she continues. "But I realized, he's part of the reason I can't ever seem to get back on my feet, you know? Like, he hasn't had a job in forever. And I don't even know what he does all day. All I know is, he takes my money, and whenever I ask him to go buy groceries or something, he says he will but then he doesn't."

"You deserve better than that," I murmur.

"Yeah. And another thing," she continues, sounding defiant. "I don't wanna work as a dancer at Jimmy Mazur's place anymore. It's where I met Mickey, anyway, and I don't wanna be part of that. Jimmy wanted me to move into... other stuff." She trails off for a second, looking embarrassed. But then she speaks up again. "Like, customers aren't supposed to touch the dancers, right? But

Jimmy started saying I could make more money if I let them do stuff sometimes..." Her nostrils flare. "I thought Mickey would kick his ass when I told him that, but you know what? He said he'd be fine with it if I could bring more money in! Can you believe that?"

"No, I can't," I say, disgusted. This is gross, even for Mickey.

"I want away from the whole thing," Bethany declares. "Yoda says he'll let us stay at his place for a little bit. Get on my feet. I said no, we can go back to the motel..." Her words slow now, as she grows hesitant. "But, I don't know how I'm gonna pay for things. I haven't been able to save up any money because of Mickey. And I haven't been working as much since Paisley's been in the hospital..."

I take a deep breath. "Bethany, we'll figure this out. For now, just take the time to relax a little bit, be glad your daughter's out of the hospital, and that you're both safe. You've got people around you now who can help."

Bailey, who's been sipping on a glass of water, announces she's going to get herself a beer. "Can I get you two anything?"

I've finished with my Coke. "I'll take another one of these," I say, lifting my glass. "With some rum in it this time, if they have it."

Bethany, after hesitating a second, asks for the same.

"You sure you can get all three drinks?" I ask Bailey. "I can help you if you'd like."

"I've got it," Bailey says, getting up. "No worries."

Bethany and I sit in comfortable silence, watching the kids play, until Bailey comes back, juggling three glasses. We take our drinks from her, and she sits back down in her spot. Bailey lifts up her beer. "To new beginnings," she announces.

"To new beginnings," I say, smiling at Bethany.

"So, Laney," Bailey continues after she's taken a sip. The corners of her mouth turn up. "Now that we've asked Bethany about her and Yoda... what's the deal with you and Rourke?"

"Um..." Now it's my turn to blush. "I plead the fifth?"

Bailey bursts out laughing. "Oh, no, you don't. You don't know me that well yet, but I am not someone who takes no for an answer." She points at my rum and Coke, smirking. "What do you think that's for? I'll ply you with liquor until you tell me!"

"It's only fair, really," Bethany pipes up with a wink. "After all, you just asked me about Yoda. And I guarantee you, things with Yoda and me haven't gone as far as whatever is going on between you and Rourke!"

The two women stare at me pointedly.

"You are not both ganging up on me right now," I protest.

They look at each other, then back at me. "Yup, I think we are," Bethany answers proudly.

"Dammit..." I glance at the little girls, but they're wrapped up in their game and aren't listening. "Sorry. Um, there's nothing going on, really..."

Bethany snorts. "Yeah, right. I've seen the two of you together. And you're here, aren't you?" She waves her arms around the clubhouse. "You can't tell me Rourke brought you here just to check up on Paisley and me."

"Well, he kind of did..." I begin, but then I remember the sound of Rourke's deep voice and the feel of his lips against my skin.

I want a replay of last night. That okay with you?

"Oh, come on. That man looks at you like you're something to eat," Bailey declares. "Don't even try to pretend there's nothing going on."

"I mean..." I start to stammer. Bailey hoots.

"I knew it!" she crows. "Okay, we've established that there *is* in fact something going on with Rourke. So. Spill!"

"He's just, um... I mean, we're just spending some time together." I lift a shoulder. "I don't think it means anything..."

The way Bailey arches her brow at me tells me she's not having it. "Laney, let me tell you something," she says. "I haven't known Rourke all that long. But I have known him long enough to know one thing: if he is spending time with you, it means something. Let me ask you a question." She leans forward. "How did you get to the clubhouse tonight?"

I tilt my head. "On Rourke's bike."

"Ha! I knew it!" She does a little fist pump, nearly spilling her beer. "In Rourke's world, that means you're practically engaged!"

I'm spared from having to answer her when the front door to the clubhouse opens up. One of the Lords who was standing near the grill earlier calls out, "Food's on! Come and get it before it's gone!"

Addi and Paisley squeal and scramble to their feet, then start running toward the door. We watch them go, laughing, then get to our feet to follow them.

In spite of myself, my heartbeat begins to speed up, knowing I'm about to see Rourke.

"Did you mean what you said about Rourke just now?" I murmur quietly to Bailey.

She turns and looks me in the eyes. "I did. Rourke is not the kind of man to get attached. I think he's a lot further gone for you than maybe even he realizes."

23

LANEY

Outside, my eyes immediately scan for Rourke. When I find him, he's already looking at me. He shoots me a sexy grin and motions for me to come to him.

"You want a steak?" he asks, wrapping his large, warm arm around me and pulling me close. "Or something else?"

"Well, since you fed me a hamburger last time, I'll go steak this time. Medium, if I have a choice."

Laughter rumbles from his throat. "We'll see if I can get Dante not to fuck it up."

A few minutes later, I'm sitting in a camping chair, eating a perfectly-prepared T-bone steak off a paper plate. My rum and Coke is sitting on the ground beside me.

"I don't know why you worried Dante wouldn't know how to cook this," I say to Rourke in between bites. "It's delicious."

"That's because I pulled it off the fire before he could destroy it."

"The hell you did," Dante calls from the other side of the grill.

"If I'd left it up to you, Laney'd be chewing on shoe leather right now," Rourke tosses back.

I listen to the men banter back and forth, polishing off my steak in record time. I haven't eaten much today, and it's nice to have some protein in my growling stomach — not to mention it's good to have something in there to sop up the rum in my Coke. When I'm finished, I lean back and sigh happily, taking in the setting sun and the sounds of the men, women, and children around me. Again, I'm struck by how strangely normal this all seems — and how nice it is. I feel full, slightly buzzed, and content, surrounded by people I barely know but still somehow trust.

"Laney."

My eyes pop open as a strong, gentle hand shakes my shoulder. "You good?"

I stare up into Rourke's eyes. The dark night sky surrounds him, sprinkled with stars.

"I must have fallen asleep," I murmur, pulling myself up in the chair. "How long was I out?"

"About an hour, maybe." Rourke's grinning at me, clearly amused.

"Wow." I blink. "I'm sorry."

"Don't be. You must have needed it."

"Where is everyone?" I ask, looking around.

"Most of them went back inside. Bailey took Addi back home. Bethany's gettin' Paisley ready for bed in Yoda's apartment."

I smile up at him apologetically. "I'm not much of a date, am I?"

"Date's not over yet, babe. Come on."

He reaches out a hand, and I take it. Rourke pulls me up to a stand and slips his arm around my waist, just like he did a few hours ago. It feels so good to have him pull me close like this. It feels safe. Warm.

I could definitely get used to it.

I find myself hoping I'll get the chance to.

My throat feels dry as we go back inside the clubhouse. The muted music I heard outside is louder now, the men talking and laughing above it as they play pool or cards, shots of whiskey and bottles of beer in front of them. A couple of them whistle and catcall as we go past, but Rourke ignores them. He takes me through the narrow hallway Bethany pointed out earlier. Toward the back, where she said some of the men have apartments.

A low ache starts between my legs when I realize where Rourke must be taking me.

"Is this the next part of our date?" I whisper.

Instead of giving me an answer, he opens a door far down on the right side of the hallway and leads me through it. Inside, he flips the switch on a lamp that's sitting on a small table just inside the door. It bathes the room in a low, warm glow, revealing a small studio apartment that's a lot nicer than I would have expected. It's sparse, and clean, with a king-sized bed off to one side of the room, under a long window through which I glimpse the same stars we were sitting under just a few minutes ago.

"Your apartment?" I ask.

Rourke nods, drawing me to him. "Yeah. I have a place in town, too, but I stay here when I'm at the clubhouse late enough that I don't want to ride home."

"You know, this is almost romantic," I tease him. I raise my arms and put them around his neck, feeling the cords of his muscles through the fabric of his shirt.

He breathes out a low rumble of laughter. "You were expecting candles and roses?"

I turn my face up to his, seeing the intensity of his gaze as it bores into me. There's no mistaking the desire in Rourke's eyes. It burns hot as fire, making my heart speed up fast as a hummingbird's in my chest. Suddenly short of breath, my lips part. I feel like I'm falling. But I know Rourke is here to catch me.

"No," I whisper. "This is what I want. Just this."

When he puts his lips to mine, its as though all the air is sucked from the room. He pulls me closer, my sex pressed hard against his hip. I moan and writhe against him, already driven nearly wild with desire. After last night, I *know* what he can do to me, and I need it, need *him* to take control of me, body and soul. My arms go tighter around his neck as he devours me, his hands lowering to cup my ass and pull me against the hard steely length of him. Oh, *God*, it's good.

Suddenly, Rourke tenses. "Fuck," he groans, but it sounds more like pain. Then it hits me.

"Oh, my God, I totally forgot you're hurt!" I cry, pulling away.

Rourke grits his teeth. "It's okay. Not that bad. I just gotta move a little differently, is all."

He pulls me back to him, his mouth on mine. Our tongues find each other. One of Rourke's hands comes up to my hair, his fingers twisting it into a rope. With a tug, he pulls my head back, exposing my neck. His mouth leaves mine, and begins its descent down the sensitive skin. The roughness of his beard contrasts with the heat of his lips, making me tremble and cling to him. The hand that was on my ass reaches under my shirt, his fingers grazing my skin. Somehow, he's unclasped my bra, and then he's cupping my breast, sliding a callused thumb against my nipple. A loud moan escapes my throat; I angle my hips upward, needing to feel more of his hardness against me, to relieve the pressure that's quickly building inside me.

Rourke raises his head and pulls away from me, taking a couple of steps back. I'm so dizzy with need I almost stumble, but manage to keep myself upright.

He shrugs out of his cut and pulls off his T-shirt with one hand, the other going to his fly. A second later, he's naked to the waist, and he's unsheathed himself, his cock hard and pulsing in his hand. I watch, paralyzed with lust and admiration, as he slowly begins to stroke. His eyes on me.

"I want to see you," he rasps.

Even though we were together last night, I've never stood in front of him naked before. But seeing him like this, huge and hard, makes me bold. I want him to look at me as he strokes himself. I want to see that it's me who's doing that to him.

My lower lip sliding between my teeth, I force myself to lock eyes with him. I unbutton my blouse, slowly, trembling. When I'm finished, I lower my arms, and the silky material slips down, onto the floor. My bra goes next until, like him, I'm naked from the waist up. Rourke's eyes leave mine, moving downward, his gaze caressing my breasts as the nipples harden from desire and the slight chill in the air.

"Jesus, Laney." His voice is thick. "Jesus fucking Christ."

I unzip my pants and let them fall to the floor, stepping out of them as well as my shoes. I stand before him now, just wearing my panties, which are soaking wet — so much so that I'm thankful the light is low.

I take a step toward him, thrumming with desire and the need to touch and be touched. When I'm standing in front of him, I reach down and encircle his cock with my hand. Rourke sucks in a breath and freezes. My fingers barely fit around him. He's incredibly hard for me, the velvet steel of him hot to the touch. Rourke takes his own hand away as I start to stroke him, mesmerized at how gorgeous he is. I've never known a man who affects me like this — never seen a man whose body I find so beautiful.

My mouth is practically watering with the need to have him in my mouth. Rourke doesn't stop me as I slowly drop to my knees. I lean forward, and see his thighs tense. Then, my tongue is sliding across the head of his cock, tasting the saltiness of his precum as I half-close my eyes.

The groan that rips from Rourke's throat sounds like a caged animal. He stiffens, one hand going to the top of my head. I lean forward and slide more of him into my mouth, my lips tightening around him. I start to move, taking him as deep as I can, and wrapping one hand around the base of his shaft to stroke him in the same rhythm.

"Laney," he murmurs. "Fuck, you feel good. I'm not gonna be able to take much of that."

My heart thrills at his words. *I'm doing this to him!*

I slow my strokes, savoring the taste and the heat of him. I never believed women enjoyed giving blow jobs — not really — and this is a revelation to me. I would do this to Rourke every day, and never get tired of it. To feel how he responds to me, hear the way his breathing goes ragged as I suck and tease him... I want to make him come like this. I want him to lose control, his legs shaking as he explodes in my mouth.

I want to be the only woman to make him feel this way.

God help me, I want to be the only woman in Rourke's life.

My thoughts are interrupted by Rourke hissing out a curse and pulling away from me.

"On the bed," he orders roughly.

I immediately do as he says. I move to the king-size bed, and I'm barely sitting down when he's moving over me, pushing me down onto my back. He props himself on one knee and takes the thin fabric of my panties in his fingers. Eyes locked on his, I prop myself on my elbows and raise my hips so he can take them off me. I'm so ready for him to be inside me that my legs fall open, but instead of him kneeling between them, he slides down further and parts my thighs with his rough hands.

My breath catches in my throat in anticipation as I realize what's about to happen.

Then, Rourke's tongue finds my clit.

My entire body jolts with a force that hits me like a flamethrower. My hips buck toward him, with a surge of need so powerful it's almost like pain. Rourke pulls back, circling around my swollen sex, grabbing my hips and holding them down so I can't move closer to him. He slows his tongue, exploring and tasting me as I writhe and moan, at once in agony and in the most delicious pleasure I've ever felt. I can barely breathe, my every movement in rhythm with his strokes, my entire body controlled by him like a puppet master pulling my strings. I moan incoherently, trying to beg him, but I can't make my mind form any words other than his name.

He leaves my clit, sliding his tongue downward to plunge deep inside me. I know I'm wet, soaking, dripping, but I'm too far gone to be embarrassed as he licks and tastes me, I just want more, more, I just want him to let me come, to give me what he knows I'm desperate for. My cries get sharper, shorter, more desperate, and then, just when I think I might actually go insane, Rourke slides his tongue out of me and sucks my clit between his lips.

I tense. Then I explode.

I cry out, gripping at the mattress. I'm falling, falling, into a place I've never been, and all I can feel is Rourke's mouth on me, my skin on fire, the blood pounding through me as my entire body ricochets through the most intense orgasm of my life. I barely register it when he moves away, lifting himself up to kneel between my thighs. But then, the velvet heat of him slides against my opening, slick with my juices, and I cry out again as my eyes fly open.

"Laney," he says hoarsely.

Then, he's inside me.

Rourke drives himself deep, gripping my hips as he pulls me onto him. His gaze is locked on mine, dark eyes blazing with an intensity I've never seen. He withdraws, then drives in again, harder, like a man possessed. I know from the tension in his face he's working to hold himself back, but that he won't last long.

Rourke expands inside me, so much that I can feel it.

His eyes close.

Then, roaring my name, he drives into me one final time and finds his release.

I SPEND the night with Rourke in his apartment.

It feels like an oasis to me here, tucked away from the rest of the world. Somehow, in the middle of a biker clubhouse, I sleep better than I have in months. I'm dead to the world until the next morning, when once again, Rourke wakes me. But this time, it's not with a hand on my shoulder.

"Rourke," I moan as he enters me from behind. I arch my back to meet him, loving the way he stretches me.

His hand comes around my waist, grabbing mine and guiding it down to my already swollen nub, He slides my middle finger through my slick juices, then begins to swirl it against me in slow lazy circles. I tense and arch further, my head falling to the side, back against his shoulder. He kisses me deeply as he continues to swirl, and begins to pump himself inside me. It's all so much, so intense, that I start to lose any sense of where I end and he begins, and soon, almost before I realize it, I'm coming, spasming around his cock as he pumps once more and empties himself deep inside me.

I've never felt so full, or so alive, or so... *loved*.

WE MUST FALL ASLEEP AGAIN, because some time later, I wake up with a start. Leaning down over the bed, I reach into my bag on the floor and pull out my phone.

"Shoot — I'm going to be late for work!" I gasp as I look at the screen.

"You need to go home before I drive you to the hospital?" Rourke asks in a gravely voice. He props himself up on one elbow as I scramble out of bed.

I do a quick calculation in my head. "No time. I'll be okay — I have a blazer hanging up in my office." I grab up the pile of my clothes on the floor. It's not ideal, but it will have to do. "Is there...?"

"Through there," Rourke rumbles, pointing to a door.

I race to the bathroom, hoping he's not staring at my naked butt, and lock myself in. I pee, get dressed, splash some water on my face, and squeeze some toothpaste on my finger from a tube in the vanity to give my teeth a quick scrub. Thankfully, I also have a toothbrush at work.

By the time I get out of the bathroom, Rourke is dressed himself. We walk through the now-deserted main room of the club-house and out the front door to Rourke's bike. I pick up the helmet and strap it on, then get on behind him and put my feet on the pegs, marveling at how second-nature this has already started to feel.

The crisp morning air blows the cobwebs from my brain. By the time we pull up in front of the hospital entrance, I'm feeling almost fully awake. A little caffeine and I should be as good as new.

"Thanks for the ride," I murmur as I hand the helmet back to Rourke.

"You're welcome." He pauses a beat. "Am I gonna see you later?"

I bite my lip. "Do you want to see me later?"

Rourke stands up from the bike and pulls me against him. I feel the heat and length of him through the fabric of his jeans, and have to stifle a moan.

"I can barely get enough of you as it is, babe," he murmurs. The heat of his breath against my skin makes me tremble. "I think you can tell how much I want to see you later."

"Then yes," I gasp, suddenly wishing like hell today was Saturday.

Rourke bends down and takes my mouth in a kiss that leaves me dizzy and panting. "Text me later."

I watch in a daze as he drives off, engine roaring. I pull in a deep breath and let it out slowly, half-sigh, half-moan. "Sweet Jesus," I whisper.

Turning, I start toward the glass front of the building entrance. As I push through the first set of doors, I glimpse a familiar figure, standing on the other side, arms crossed.

It's Blake Barber.

And he does not look happy.

24

ROURKE

After I drop Laney off at the hospital, I'm planning to head back to my place, but a text from Axel calls me back to the clubhouse.

"Hey, what's up?" I ask him as I stride into his office. He's staring at the wall, jaw tense, hands steepled in front of him. I sit down in the straight-backed chair across from him, the legs squeaking in protest as they slide against the floor.

"I got a call from Chaco's right-hand man, Indio."

I'm instantly alert. "How's Chaco?"

"He's okay. I mean, he ain't okay, but he'll live." Axel's forehead is furrowed.

"But?"

"But." He blows out a breath. "It's about what we already figured. The ambush was the Caballeros. One of the bodies they found was a guy they recognized as a member of that gang."

"Fuck."

"Fuck is right." Axel runs a hand roughly through his hair. "Indio confirmed what Chaco said yesterday: They got enough product from a different source to get us our shipment today. But that's just a temporary fix. The fact is, Dos Santos is on the verge of a full-blown turf war."

"What do you think Angel's gonna say?" I frown.

"Don't know. I'm callin' him later today." Axel grimaces. "We got an agreement with Chaco. And Angel's a man of his word. But if Los Caballeros has turned against the Dos Santos cartel, they just lost their only ally against Sinaloa." He pauses a beat. "And we just lost our pipeline."

My head starts to pound. This is big. It ain't just the pipeline. It's our livelihoods. And more than that, it's about maintaining our hold on our territory. The Lords are going to have to make some tough decisions going forward.

"We got any other sources we could tap to fill the holes, for now?" I ask. "What about that club to the east of Angel's chapter? The Death Devils? You think they got any connections we could use?"

Axel considers for a second, then nods. "Maybe."

"Ain't one of Angel's men married to the daughter of their prez?"

"Huh. I don't know about that. But I know Angel and the prez of the Death Devils are solid." Axel sits up in his chair. "I'll talk to Angel about it. Fuck I'm not looking forward to this conversation."

"Angel ain't gonna be pissed at our club. This ain't about us. Fuck, we're lucky we all got out alive."

"Yeah. Anyway, for now Indio gave me the new location of the drop-off. So we got a few days before we have to worry about it."

"You need me to go on the run?" I ask.

"Nah. I got Dante on it. He's got enough men to go with him." For the first time, some semblance of humor appears on Axel's face. "How's your ass, anyway?"

I snort. "It's still attached to me."

"Good to know. So, what's the story with bringin' that hospital chick here last night?" he says then, lifting his chin toward the door.

"Laney? Yeah. I brought here to see the kid and her mom. Figured she'd wanna know they're safe."

"You sure it was a good idea? She seems kind of... straight arrow." He huffs out a laugh. "Never would have taken her for the type to wanna take a walk on the wild side, you know?"

"She ain't as buttoned up as you'd think."

"Never would've taken you for the type to go for a chick like that, either."

I bristle. "What's that supposed to mean?"

"Aw, calm the fuck down, Rourke. You know what I mean. You seem to like your chicks... easy, for lack of a better word. Uncomplicated." He shakes his head. "That gash? She looks like a motherfuckin' complication. Too much fuckin' effort for pussy, if you ask me."

His words broadside me completely. A wave of fury rises up inside me, making me want to leap out of my chair and fuckin' waste his ass. My fists clench tight against my thighs. My prez notices.

"I hit a nerve?" he asks mildly.

"No," I lie, my jaw tensing. Blood starts rushing in my ears.

Axel bursts out laughing, throwing his head back as he slides back into his chair. "You're a fuckin' pathetic liar, brother. You're about a second away from kickin' my ass. Not that you could."

"Jesus," I hiss, clenching my fists harder. "You really want to head down the path to where this is gonna end up?"

Axel raises his hands. "Naw, brother. I just wanted to figure out how far gone you were for this chick." He chuckles. "Looks like the answer is, pretty fuckin' far."

"Yeah, well, that's my business," I growl.

A tap on the door jamb interrupts us. Scowling, I turn, just looking for an excuse to beat someone's head in. It's Yoda. He frowns, looking from me to Axel, then back at me.

"Shit, what the hell did I interrupt?" he asks.

"Nothing," I growl. Axel just laughs.

"Uh, okay," Yoda says dubiously. "So, Rourke, I'm gonna go take Bethany to get her car. She wants to take Paisley back to school this afternoon. Then I guess she's gonna go over to the hospital to talk to Laney about some shit."

"Okay," I grunt. "Thanks for letting me know." Roughly, I push back the chair I'm in and stand. "We done here?" I shoot at Axel.

He smirks. "Sure thing, brother."

I flash him an angry glare, then turn and brush past Yoda and out of the office. I've had enough of my brothers meddling in my business for today. I don't need to stick around and give Yoda a chance to start in, too.

I'm muttering to myself as I make my way out the door of the clubhouse. My plan is to head back to my place, grab a shower, and then take the bike out on a long ride somewhere out of town. I need to clear my head for a while. And there's nothing better for that than the open road.

Because as fucking pissed off as I am right now, I have to admit, Axel was right when he said he hit a nerve.

Outside, I straddle the seat of my Harley and fire it up. The deep rumble of the engine under me is as familiar as my own heartbeat.

Having Laney at the clubhouse last night and this morning felt... good. Natural, even. You wouldn't really think Laney would fit in here, but somehow, she did. And I liked having her here, with me. Seeing here there, shooting the shit with Gage's old lady. It was like she belonged.

Like she could belong to *me*.

I don't quite know what to make of this. I never saw it coming.

Or hell, maybe I'm lying to myself. Maybe I've wanted this all along. I don't know.

All I know is, I want to keep seeing Laney. I want her on the back of my bike.

I want her under me. I want her on top of me. I want her every way and any way I can have her.

My cock stirs.

Jesus. I think I'm gonna have to do something about this.

BACK AT MY PLACE, I'm out of the shower, a towel wrapped around my waist, when I notice there's a new message on my phone. It's from Joe McBride, his personal cell.

I don't bother to listen to the message, just press reply pull the phone up to my ear.

"Hey," I say as soon as he answers. "I saw you called."

"Yeah. Just wanted to give you a heads up. Mickey King's out on bond. His hearing was this morning. Judge set the bond at a thousand dollars, and someone bailed him out."

"You happen to get the name of the person?"

"Yeah. A James Mazur."

Huh. So Jimmy Mazur loaned Mickey the money. I wonder what Mickey had to promise him in exchange.

"Sucks that he's out," I remark, "but good to know. Thanks for tellin' me. You got anything else?"

"Just his court date."

Joe tells me when it is, but I'm not all that interested. Mickey might get jail time, he might not. My only concern is making sure I know his whereabouts from now until then. And making sure he leaves Paisley and her mom the fuck alone.

I thank Joe and hang up, then get dressed. I call Yoda and leave him a message, letting him know Mickey's out. After that, I head out on my ride, thinking I might take a detour back over to Jimmy Mazur's place on the way back. See if he knows what hole Mickey has crawled into.

25

LANEY

"Laney."

Blake Barber's voice is dry as a husk.

Final.

Definitive.

"I need to see you in my office. Now."

A few minutes later, I'm perched in the impossibly uncomfortable chair that sits across from him, looking at him over the expanse of his desk. I swear he chose this thing on purpose, just to make it suck more to be in here.

I haven't had the chance to talk to Katie about whether Blake has questioned her yet. But given my presence in his office right now, my assumption is that he has. And that she had to throw me under the bus to protect her own job. So, as I sit in silence, waiting for Blake to speak, I steel myself for the worst.

I'm going to be questioned, and I'm going to have to give him the version of the story I've crafted in my mind. The one where Katie had absolutely nothing to do with trapping Mickey. I hope my acting chops are up to the task.

But as it turns out, Blake has called me in here for a completely different reason.

"I CANNOT fathom why you are consorting with an obvious criminal, Laney," he states, his mouth twisted with contempt.

I expect him to say more, but apparently he thinks that's enough. And that apparently, he also thinks I owe him some sort of explanation for showing up on the back of Rourke's bike just now.

"Excuse me... what?" I squint at him in disbelief.

"I have to tell you that I am extremely shocked and disappointed in you," he says sternly.

I can't believe what I'm hearing. "Are you asking me to answer to you for what I choose do to on my own time?" I gape at him.

"It certainly makes me question your judgment," he sniffs, pursing his lips. "And also makes me question your motives."

I'm not sure where this is heading, but I don't like it one bit. "Motives? Motives about what? What are you talking about, Blake?"

He narrows his eyes, for just a moment.

"Delaney, you are an employee of this hospital," Blake drones. "You have access to privileged information, and your integrity needs to be absolutely above question." He's chosen the sanctimonious air he uses when he wants to pull rank on an employee. "When I see you spending time with a man who clearly comes from the lowest rungs of society, I can only come to one of two conclusions. Either you are too stupid to realize he is playing you... or you are not too stupid. In which case, I have to assume you approve of, or even participate in, his criminal activity."

My whole body stiffens with anger. "I absolutely resent those implications," I shoot back. "Both about me, and about Rourke."

"Aha. So you *are* too stupid to see it." He shakes his head in exaggerated display of sadness.

My heart is racing. My head is pounding. In less than ten

seconds, I've gone from nervous but resolved, to angrier than I can remember being in years. Maybe in my life.

"How dare you?" I hiss, half-rising from my chair. "You have no right to talk to me this way. Employee or not!"

"Delaney, you are putting the safety of our employees and our patients at risk by having contact with that *biker*." He says the word like it's a disease. "I will not have that at my hospital." He leans forward, all pretense of above-it-all sanctimony gone. His eyes are blazing now — with anger, and something else that I only now am starting to see.

Jealousy.

Slowly, I start to understand. This is all about me rebuffing Blake's advances. The fact that not only have I rejected him — but even worse, that I chose an outlaw biker over him — is a bigger blow to Blake Barber's self-esteem than he can stand.

He intends to punish me for it. To salvage his own ego.

"You will promise me, right now. *Right now*, do you hear me?" His voice shakes with barely-concealed rage, as he bites off each word. "You will cease all contact with that biker. Both inside this hospital and out of it."

He stops speaking, glaring at me over his desk. It's clear he expects me to speak. To grovel.

But somehow, his fury ends up having the opposite effect on me.

My heart is still pounding, my skin abuzz with adrenaline. But strangely, I feel calm. Absolutely calm.

"I will not promise that," I say quietly. "And I expect an apology from you. Right now."

"An apology from *me*?" Blake bursts into incredulous laughter. "Are you out of your mind?"

"No?" I put my hands on the armrests of the impossibly uncomfortable chair and stand up. "Well, then. I quit. Effective immediately."

He flinches, and then blinks, as though he's not sure what he's just heard.

"You can't be serious," he says uncertainly. His face is still fixed in the same stern expression, but his body posture has collapsed.

I've stunned him. Outplayed him.

"I am serious. I'm not your slave, Blake." I wait a beat. "And I'm not your girlfriend, either. And never will be. *That biker*, as you call him, is twice the man you'll ever be. And there's nothing you could ever do or say to make me think any differently about that. Or him."

I lean over the desk, until my face is just inches from his.

"I'm done with your bullshit, Blake. You're a shitty boss, and a shitty human being. And one more thing: I suggest that you count your blessings that I'm not bringing sexual harassment charges against you. *Yet*."

I pause for a second, to let my words sink in. Then, I take a deep breath.

"I also want you to know that I'm quite aware I'm not the only woman on staff here at the hospital you've made unwanted advances toward. Your record as regards your female employees is abysmal. Women talk, Blake. We talk about how you treat us. You've made a lot of enemies here. And up until now, you probably thought none of your bad behavior would bite you in the ass.

"I'm not sure if you know this," I continue, "but my father is Senator Rodney Hart, from Kentucky. I certainly have the means to assemble quite a legal team against you. And as it turns out, he's quite friendly with the senior senator from Ohio. So..." I pause again. "I suggest you treat your staff — *all* of your staff — with nothing but the utmost respect and professionalism going forward. Especially the ones who are likely to talk to me after I leave here. Do you understand?"

Blakes eyes are wide. He hasn't moved a muscle.

He swallows. I watch as his Adam's apple bobs.

"Goodbye, Blake."

Without waiting for an answer, I straighten myself to my full height, turn, and walk out of his office.

Inside my brain, I'm doing a whoop of victory, even as part of me wonders what the hell I just did.

I very well may have just committed career suicide. But it's done now.

And damn, did it feel good.

I exit Blake's office, doing a mental victory dance. Instead of heading to my office, I decide to go find Katie. I want to tell her I'm pretty sure Blake will drop the matter of Mickey following her into the med closet, and why. And also, I want to make sure she hears the news that I'm leaving from me before anyone else.

Unfortunately, when I get up to the nurses station on the second floor, I remember that today's her day off. I chat for a few minutes with Megan, one of the nurses on duty, not letting on that there's anything unusual. Then I go back to my office to start cleaning out my desk, still on a high of adrenaline and righteous pride. I'll call Katie later, and tell her the news.

It's only when my cell phone rings and I check the screen that it hits me how badly I've just screwed up.

"Hi, Bethany," I answer, my voice suddenly sounding very far away in my head.

"Laney! I'm so sorry to ask you this, but I really need help. Mickey just stole my car again!"

"What?" I gasp.

"I'm at the motel where we were staying. I came back here to settle the bill before dropping Paisley off at school this afternoon. Turns out, the manager kicked Mickey out of the room because he didn't think Mickey would pay. So, I go to the manager's office, to find out what he did with our stuff, and when I come back out with Paisley, my car's gone!"

I feel ill, but do my best to conceal it. "Are you sure Mickey did it?"

"I mean, I didn't see him do it, but he's the only one who has a key besides me." Her voice rises a notch. "He must be out of jail!"

"Shit!"

"Yeah, shit is right," she agrees. "So I'm sitting here with Paisley now, with no transportation. And I can't get hold of Yoda. Look, Laney, I hate to ask this, but could you come pick me up? I figure since I was supposed to come by the hospital anyway to talk to you, maybe it wouldn't be too much of an inconvenience? I can figure out a ride from the hospital afterwards."

"Sure, I'll come get you," I murmur, the words coming out strangled.

"Are you sure?" Bethany asks, misunderstanding my tone. "I mean, if you can't come get us, it's okay, I can figure something out."

"No, no. I'll be there soon. Sit tight."

I sit back in my desk chair, feeling numb and horrified. Stunned, I log out of my computer and pack up my few personal items, a heavy lump in the pit of my stomach. When I'm finished, I pick up the box of my belongings and pull my office door closed.

Then I walk down the hall, my mind desperately trying to figure out how I'm going to break the news to Bethany. The news I've only just realized myself.

Now that I'm no longer an employee of Morningside Hospital, I don't have access to the resources to help her.

I 'm feeling sick to my stomach when I pull up in front of the motel. Bethany and Paisley are sitting on the curb in the parking lot, in front of a wooden staircase that leads up to the second floor. Next to Paisley is a tiny battered pink rolling suitcase. On Bethany's other side are two large garbage bags, stuffed full.

I say hello to the two of them and pop the trunk. I help them load their stuff in the back, hoping they don't ask about the paper ream box of my stuff that's back there already. Thankfully, they don't seem to notice it.

As I turn the car out of the parking lot, Bethany frowns. "Aren't we going to the hospital?"

"Um... I thought we'd be more comfortable talking at my house," I stammer, stalling for time. "Plus, it's almost lunch time. Do you want to come over for grilled cheese or something? I could take you and Paisley over to the school after that."

"Yeah!" Paisley yells from behind us, clearly enthused about the grilled cheese part.

I laugh. "Well, that's a yes from the back seat. You good with that?"

"Sure," Bethany agrees with a smile. "It'll be fun to see where you live."

I find myself driving slower than usual. Probably because subconsciously, I'm trying to prolong the inevitable. *I'll tell Bethany after lunch. Or maybe after we've dropped off Paisley.*

Bethany launches into an animated account of getting back their things from the motel manager as I drive. "So first, he says he threw all our stuff in the Dumpster. Then, while I was trying to get him to tell me how many days I owed him for, he lets it slip that he was planning to sell some of our stuff to make up the money I owed. So of course, I say, 'Wait a minute, so you mean to tell me you've got my stuff after all? I am not paying you one penny until you bring it out here and I see that every single thing is there!' So then, he realized he'd better give me my sh... stuff. Cause it sure as heck isn't worth hundreds of dollars, no matter where he tries to sell it!"

I'm listening with half an ear. "What a jerk," I mumble.

"You're tellin' me. Frankly, I got the feeling he was trying to work up the guts to ask about me payin' him back in *other ways*, if you get my drift." Bethany's eyes flit back to Paisley. "What a loser," she finishes, disgusted.

"So, did you settle up with him?" I ask.

Bethany shrugs. "I gave him two-hundred dollars and told him to take it or leave it. It cleared out my checking account, but at least I'm finished with him."

We've arrived at my house. I pull into the driveway, then help Paisley out of the back seat as her mom continues chattering. I leave the box of my stuff in the trunk for now. I can get it after I've dropped Paisley off at school and taken Bethany wherever she needs to go.

I can only blame my troubled thoughts and Bethany's distraction for what happens next.

For not paying attention as we go up the walk together.

For not hearing the engine of another car as it pulls up outside.

For me leaving the front screen door unlocked on an unseasonably warm fall day.

"SO, GRILLED CHEESE IT IS!" I say brightly. "You have a choice of cheddar or provolone, Miss Paisley."

Paisley wrinkles her nose. "What's provolone?"

"She's good with cheddar," Bethany says, sinking into a chair at my tiny kitchen table. "On the other hand, this crazy kid likes wheat bread more than white. Go figure."

"Wow. That is crazy." I pull out the bread and a pan and get to work on lunch. "So, Paisley," I ask, "Are you happy to get back to school?"

I almost hesitate to ask the question, knowing that Paisley has had a rough time with some of her classmates. But to my surprise, she bobs her head excitedly and flashes a grin.

"Addi's mom says when we get to school we're supposed to ask where her room is, so I can find it if I ever need to go talk to her. And also she said she can start driving me home after school so me and Addi can play in her classroom until she's done working."

"Bailey's been so nice," Bethany sighs. "I can't believe she's okay with taking care of Paisley after school. It sure will help me while I start looking for another job."

"That's great!" And it really is. God, things really seem like maybe they're starting to pick up for the two of them. Funny, it seems like it's all because of the MC, directly or indirectly.

Ironically, the only part that isn't going great is the part *I* was supposed to be taking care of.

I set some buttered bread in the pan that's heating on the stove, and start to slice pieces of cheese to lay on top.

"Do you need any help?" Bethany asks, starting to rise from her chair.

"No, I—"

A loud crash from the front of the house interrupts me, making all three of us jump.

"Where the fuck are you?" a high, angry male voice booms.

Paisley lets out a small scream, claps her hand to her mouth, and clings to her mother.

Dammit! I don't know how we didn't notice, but he must have followed us here. Turning off the burner in disgust, I throw down the knife and stomp toward the living room, shouting, "Mickey, you get out of my house right n—"

Which is when I come face to face with the barrel of a gun.

Mickey points the thing at me, shoving it toward me. I back up towards the kitchen, almost stumbling on the threshold. When Paisley sees him, she screams again and buries her face in her mother's shoulder.

"Mickey, what the hell are you doing here?" Bethany yells.

"You shut the fuck up, bitch!" He waves the gun over toward her. I feel sick, half-expecting it to go off any second. Mickey's an excitable type, but I've never seen him like this. His eyes are open far too wide, the whites showing, and his movements are jerky and erratic. He smells like sour sweat.

"You stole my car!" Bethany accuses, narrowing her eyes at him.

"You didn't fuckin' bail me out!" Mickey screams. "You didn't fuckin' bail me out! You left me in that jail to rot! You fuckin' bitch! You fuckin' bitch!"

"Why should I bail you out, Mickey?" Bethany yells right back at him. "You were the one stupid enough to try to steal drugs from a goddamn hospital! We are over, Mickey! I'm not your fucking doormat anymore!"

I've never seen her like this, either. For the first time since I met Bethany, she doesn't seem afraid of Mickey. Which, considering the situation, worries me. It seems evident to me that he could go off at any minute — that this gun in his hand, if it's loaded, could kill any one of us. Maybe all of us.

I start to feel dizzy. Weakly, I slide into an unoccupied kitchen chair.

"You're comin' with me to see Mazur!" Mickey yells at Bethany. "Thanks to you, I had to borrow money from him to bail me out! He's gonna come after me unless I pay him back."

"That's your problem!" Bethany shoots back. "I ain't got any money anyway! You took everything I had!"

"You're gonna work it off, bitch," Mickey seethes, narrowing his eyes. "And you're gonna start right the fuck now."

This isn't going to end well. Mickey's not going to leave without Bethany. And Bethany, bless her heart, seems to have finally grown the backbone to stand up to him once and for all. Mickey's eyes are wide and unfocused as he shouts at all of us, the gun in his hand waving wildly. Any second now, his finger could slip. There's nothing I can do — no way for me to get to him before he'd have time to take aim at me and pull the trigger.

"Mickey." I cut in, speaking as calmly as I can although my voice is shaking. "You really need to leave now. Take Bethany's car. You can sell it or something, to get the money. Just leave her and Paisley alone." I shoot Bethany a look that I hope says, *Let's just say whatever it takes to get him out of here.*

But Mickey's wounded pride seems to have made him almost crazy. "You shut up, you fuckin' cunt!" he shouts at me. He opens his mouth to say more, but then suddenly stops. Narrowing his eyes, a malicious grin transforms his features.

"You're comin' with us," he sneers. "You and your fuckin' ATM card."

Bethany speaks up again. "We are not coming with you, Mickey. I already told you that."

"And *this* says you are!" Mickey lifts the gun and aims it at her head. At the last second, he raises it, points it at the wall behind her, and fires.

Paisley screams and begins to sob uncontrollably. I stifle the cry that's lodged in my throat.

"Now get the fuck up and come on!" Micky shouts.

I don't think we have a choice. We have to go with Mickey. At least for now. I'm no longer sure he won't use the gun on us if he feels he has to. We're alone, unarmed. No one will be able to help us. Desperately, I try to think of some way to get us out of this.

And then, suddenly, out of the blue, the ghost of an idea comes to me.

It's not much of one, but it's all I have.

Clinging to a desperate hope, I start to move my arm, as slowly as I can, so Mickey won't notice any movement. He's pointing the gun at Bethany and Paisley, watching them as they rise from their chairs and come around the table. My eyes still locked on him, I reach into my blazer pocket. I thumb my cell phone ringer to silent, then move to the volume button and hold it until I'm sure it's down all the way. As Mickey continues to yell at Bethany, I keep my motions as small as possible, slipping the phone out of my pocket. Under the table, I take quick, furtive glances at the screen out of the corner of my eye, until I manage to find the number I want in my contacts, and press it.

I slip my phone back in the pocket, praying Mickey won't hear it ringing on the other end.

The heel of my hand is over the earpiece, so I barely catch the muffled voice when he answers. I wait a second or two, then take a deep breath and break into Bethany and Mickey's argument.

"Mickey," I say loudly, hearing my voice shake. "I know you're angry at Bethany, but breaking into my house with a loaded gun and threatening us is not the answer."

"I told you to shut up, bitch!" he spits at me.

I try again, wanting to make sure Rourke can hear what's happening, and that he knows where we are.

"How did you find my house, Mickey? How did you know where I live?"

"I didn't." He sneers at me, showing his overly-large teeth. "You dumb bitches. I followed you from the motel. You didn't even see my car."

"*My* car," Bethany mutters. Mickey looks like he's going to explode at her. I try to make eye contact with her, try to signal to her to back down, but her eyes are locked on him.

"Mickey, look," I say. "Please, for the last time. You need to put away that gun and leave my house. Right now. And let us go. Please don't kidnap us in Bethany's car."

"The fuck I will!" he yells. He turns to me, spittle flying from his mouth. "Get up outta that chair. Move!"

Next to Bethany, poor Paisley is still sobbing and trembling like a leaf. I'm afraid to press my luck at this point, but decide to try one more time to get my message across to the person I hope is listening on the other end of the phone. "Where are you taking us, Mickey?"

"First of all, you are gonna clean out your bank account for me," he sneers. "So get the fuck up, *now!* And no more talkin', or I put a bullet in your head as soon as I get that goddamn money."

I stand up, so shaky that I almost stumble. Numbly, I follow Bethany and Paisley out the front door, terrified Mickey will completely lose control of his temper or accidentally pull the trigger and kill one of us. I don't dare talk anymore.

Mickey orders all three of us in the front seat of the car. He gets into the back, and tells all of us to stay quiet and keep facing forward. He directs Bethany to drive to the nearest bank and pull into an ATM drive-though.

I don't have any idea what happens after I get Mickey the money from my bank account. I have no idea whether he'll take me with them, or leave me on the side of the road, or do something worse. What I do know is he's not thinking all that clearly — and that he might be on drugs. And he's so angry, it's almost impossible to predict what he'll do next.

One thing is certain. I can't let him separate me from Bethany and Paisley. No matter what happens, I won't leave them.

I just have to stall, keep looking for an opening, and pray.

Pray that Rourke heard me.

And pray that he gets to us in time.

27

ROURKE

T urns out, that ride I was planning to go on doesn't happen.

I'm out in my driveway, trying to decide how to time it so I'll end up in a good place for lunch, when my phone rings. Grumbling, I pull it out of my pocket, hoping it ain't Axel calling me back to the clubhouse. But instead, it's Laney.

She's never called me before. Not sure what she'd be calling about, since I just saw her a couple hours ago, but I sure as hell don't mind seeing her name on the screen. I accept the call and pull the phone up to my ear.

"Hey," I say.

But on the other end, no voice greets me back. Instead, it's a muffle of sounds. Almost like it's under water. The kind of noise you get when someone butt dials you.

"Well, fuck," I snort.

I'm deciding whether to hang up or to shout into the phone, to let her know she called me by mistake. Just when I figure I might as well end the call, Laney's unmistakeable voice comes through the earpiece. Muted, but definitely her.

"Mickey, I know you're angry at Bethany, but breaking into my house with a loaded gun and threatening us is not the answer."

"You can fuck off, bitch!" someone in the background yells.

Mickey.

"How did you find my house, Mickey? How did you know where I live?" Laney asks. Her voice is clear as a bell. Almost as though she knows I'm on the line and she's trying to make sure I hear it.

Which... fuck, which of course she is!

"I didn't. You dumb bitches," Mickey's voice shoots back. He says something else after that, but I can't make it out.

"Mickey, look," I hear then. "Please, for the last time. You need to put away that gun and leave my house. Right now. And let us go. Please don't kidnap us in Bethany's car."

Jesus fuck. Mickey's at her house. And he's got a gun. And Bethany and Paisley are there with her.

It's the hardest goddamn thing I've ever done to hang up that call. But I can't risk having Mickey hear any noise from my end and realize Laney's contacted someone outside the house. Heart in my throat, I punch in Yoda's number and just about go out of my goddamn mind waiting until he answers.

"Yoda!" I yell as I fire up my engine. "Mickey's got Bethany and Laney! He's at Laney's house, and he's got a gun on them! Where you at?"

"Clubhouse!" Yoda yells back. "Fuck, what's the address?"

I tell him. "Get there now. But keep an eye on Bethany's car! I'm pretty sure he's plannin' to kidnap them!"

Following the speed limit, it takes about eight minutes to get from my house to Laney's. I make it in just over four.

I'm the first Lord to make it there. Laney's car is out front, but it's the only one. "Fuck!" I yell. I practically dump my bike next to the curb and run up the short hill of steps to Laney's place. I push through the unlocked screen door, yanking my gun out of my waistband. "Laney!" I yell, my voice booming through the house. "Laney!"

I'm met with silence. The living room is deserted. I go into the kitchen. There's an open loaf of bread on the counter, and a block of cheese. A skillet is sitting on the stove with a piece of bread in it. It smells like gunpowder in here. I look around, scanning, and finally up at the far wall.

A bullet hole.

My stomach roils as I hear motorcycle engines approach outside. I turn and run back out the door in time to see Yoda pull up with Rogue and Mal.

"We just missed them!" I shout. "This is Laney's car, so they must have taken Bethany's! There's a bullet hole in the wall, but I didn't see any blood."

Yoda pulls out his phone and holds it up to me. "The tracker I put on her car is still there. They ain't gone far! Looks like they're only a mile or so away. Car's stopped right now." He peers at the screen. "I think there's a bank on that corner."

"I'm guessing they're on their way out of town somewhere! Maybe to Mazur's place." I pause, my mind going a hundred directions at once. "We gotta hope he hasn't hurt anyone yet."

"We can intercept them, if that's where they're goin'," Yoda barks. "Wait until they get outside the city limits and surround them."

"I'll call Axel," Rogue says, grabbing his own cell. "Have him send a couple brothers out that way to meet us."

"No!" I counter, stopping them both. "Mickey's the vindictive type. The type to shoot them if he sees us coming. We gotta ambush him. We can't give him time to hurt them before we nab him."

"Wait," Yoda frowns, staring at his phone. "Holy shit! They're coming back this way."

What the fuck? "Okay, shit, get out of here before they see us! You guys go around back."

We run to the bikes, and Yoda and Rogue peel out. I follow them just around the corner, park mine out of sight, then run behind a detached garage next door to Laney's place, praying the owners are at work.

A minute later, Bethany's car pulls up. She gets out the driver's side, and then a second later the passenger door opens. Laney steps out, followed by Paisley.

Then Mickey emerges from the back seat.

He barks something at them, and the two women and the girl file up the walk, their bodies stiff, staring straight ahead. Laney opens the door, and they go inside.

I pull my gun from my waistband but hold off on thumbing off the safety. I want to deal with this without bullets unless I absolutely have to.

I zig across the yard on the grass, so my boots won't sound on the pavement and warn Mickey I'm here. Ducking under the large window to Laney's front room, I strain forward to listen.

From here, I can't make out any words. I hear Bethany's voice, though. Then, Mickey's louder, sharper one in response.

My boots aren't made for sneaking, so I slip them off and slide up onto the front stoop.

The voices I'm hearing aren't close enough to come from the living room. The next logical place they could be is back in the kitchen. You can't see the front door from there, which works in my favor. Slowly, I stick my head around the jamb of the open front door, ready to fire if I have to. Sure enough, there's no one in sight.

Pulling myself up into a crouch, I glide across the threshold and into the living room. The voices are a little louder here, and more distinct. Mickey's shouting, sounding agitated. I move toward the kitchen, still silent, my eyes scanning all around me to make sure Mickey didn't bring anyone with him.

Paisley sees me first. She's sitting at the kitchen table near the wall, her mother to her right. I barely see Mickey's arm. He's standing on the other side of the table in the middle of the room, his back to me.

Paisley's eyes meet mine, and I shake my head rapidly once. *No.* She blinks, then turns back to Mickey, expression unchanged. *Good girl.*

I move forward, toward the hallway outside the kitchen. From this vantage, I can see all of Mickey from behind. In his right hand is the gun.

Laney is in a chair on the other side of the table. Facing him.

I shove my gun back into the waistband of my jeans. From this angle, if I try to shoot Mickey, I'm liable to hit one of the women or Paisley instead. Slowly, slowly, I move further down the hall.

When Laney's face comes into view, the only way I can tell she's seen me is an almost imperceptible widening of her eyes. She freezes for an instant, then exhales slightly.

"Mickey," she says, clearing her throat. "I have to go to the bathroom."

"You think I give a shit?" he sneers. "Shut the fuck up."

"Mickey," Bethany pipes up, " Please! You're scaring Paisley! Please, put the gun away, before you hurt someone!"

"Shut up goddamnit!" he snarls. Turning to Laney, he barks, "Where's some tape or rope or somethin'?"

"There's some tape in the junk drawer," Laney says in a trembling voice. "The one over there on the far left."

Mickey inches toward that side of the kitchen, his gun still trained on the women.

"You don't need to tie me up," Laney continues. "Just leave, Mickey. You do that, and I won't say anything. No one will follow you. You have some money now. Take Bethany's car. We'll all pretend this didn't happen. It's the best thing for everyone. You can't win this way. You know that."

"Goddamnit, shut the fuck up!" Mickey yells. His back to me, he raises the gun and points it toward the ceiling.

Seeing my opening, I launch myself toward him just as the gun goes off.

The explosion is deafening in the small kitchen. I see rather than hear Mickey's piece clatter to the floor as I tackle him to the ground. His head must make a noise when it smacks against the linoleum, too, because I see the bounce. Then I'm on him, pinning him down on his stomach. I wrench both hands behind his back and look up toward the women just in time to see Bethany grab Paisley and drag her under the table.

"It's okay, it's good!" I call into the sudden silence, my voice too loud. "He's down. It's okay."

There's a shout from the living room, and the loud echo of footsteps. "Rourke!"

"Here!"

Yoda appears in the doorway. Behind the table, Bethany and Paisley are getting to their feet. Bethany picks up Paisley in her arms and runs to Yoda, sobbing. Laney stands up shakily from her chair.

Rogue pushes through and looks around the room, then down at Mickey, who's struggling and yelling. I grab his hair and knock his head once, hard, on the floor. He shuts up.

"He alone?" Rogue asks.

"Yeah. It's under control."

He nods, then looks at my feet.

"Nice socks, brother," he remarks.

"Fuck you," I toss back. Then, remembering Paisley's here, I glance at Bethany. "Sorry."

Bethany bursts out into tears. "I think you get a pass on swearing today," she says, laugh-crying.

I turn to Rogue. "Grab this motherfucker." I pull Mickey to his feet and wrench up on his arm once, hard, to let him know not to try anything. When Rogue's got a good hold on him, I move away, grab the gun off the floor, and stand.

When I look at Laney, she's smiling at me, tears shining in her eyes.

"I knew you'd figure it out," she whispers. "I knew you'd come."

I cross the room in two steps and pull her to me. "You did good, darlin'," I murmur. "I'm proud of you. You know how to think on your feet."

"Yeah?" she half-sobs. "You have any idea how I could market that skill? Because as it turns out, it looks like I'm on the job market."

"What?"

Laney sighs out a shaky laugh. "I'll explain later. For now, what are we going to do about him?" she asks, nodding at Mickey.

"Oh, don't you worry about that," I growl. "Mickey's done harassing Bethany. Or anyone else around here. I can guarantee it."

From the way Yoda's looking down at Bethany right now, I'm pretty sure he's gonna want to be the one to give Mickey the beat-down of his life. There's no doubt in my mind that this is the last time we'll be seeing Mickey King anywhere near Ironwood.

I almost feel sorry for the pathetic piece of shit. For the next twenty-four hours or so, he's gonna be sorry to be alive.

Rogue grabs the tape Mickey was gonna use to tie up Laney, binds Mickey's feet and hands, and pulls him out the side door to the attached garage. Yoda makes a quick call to one of the other brothers, gives him Laney's address, and tells him to bring a van. Then, with a nod to all of us, he leads Bethany and Paisley out of the house, toward her car, and they drive away.

I take Laney by the hand.

"Tell you what," I say. "Let's you and me take off for a while. Let these guys take it from here."

She looks around and lets out a breath. "I guess I don't want to be here for this part, do I?"

"Nope."

I lead Laney out of the house and toward my bike.

"Do I want to know what's going to happen to Mickey?" Laney asks, looking up at me apprehensively.

"Probably not," I admit. "But don't worry. He'll live."

Just barely.

28

LANEY

"So, yeah," I sigh as the waitress sets our plates in front of us. "I basically don't have a job now."

I'm trying to act normal and nonchalant, but my hands are still shaking a little bit as I pick up my burger. It wasn't even two hours ago that Mickey was waving a gun in my face and I was fearing for my life. Now, even though my mind knows I'm safe, my body doesn't seem to have quite gotten the memo yet. I was trembling on the back of Rourke's bike all the way here.

We're back at Shooter's. Rourke insisted we leave my house while the other Lords were taking care of business. Since I hadn't eaten lunch yet, he said I needed to get some food in me to help calm me down and asked me where I wanted to go.

For some reason, the first place I thought of was here.

"So you quit?" Rourke frowns. "I thought you liked working at the hospital?"

Instead of answering right away, I lean forward and bite into my burger, then close my eyes in ecstasy as the delicious, fatty goodness fills my mouth. "Oh, my God," I mumble around the mouthful. "How do they make these things so good?" I thought

I'd lost my appetite, but somehow this is the perfect comfort food.

I'm starting to think that maybe Shooter's is my happy place.

As I sit across from Rourke, trying to calm my jumbled nerves, I can't help but think back to our first date here. I almost start laughing at the thought. The word "date" is such a strange concept, when Rourke is part of the equation. Almost like him giving me his class ring, or something.

The image is enough to make me snort.

"Um, nice snort," he says.

"Thanks."

"Laney, come on," he frowns. "Talk to me. I need to know what happened at the hospital to make you quit."

I'm not quite sure how to tell him the real reason. Or if I even want to.

"Long story," I stall. "Let's just say I reached the end of my rope."

He looks like he wants to ask me for more, but thankfully he doesn't press it just yet. "Okay," he sighs. "So... what are you gonna do now?"

"I'm not sure," I admit. "That question's too hard right now. This burger, on the other hand, is *everything*." I take another bite and try not to moan out loud. "The fact is, I don't know how many other social work jobs there are in the area." A pang of remorse hits me in the chest. "Plus, not only have I just given up one of the only decent jobs around here for me, but I've also screwed Paisley and Bethany over in the balance."

"What do you mean?" he asks, raising a brow.

"I mean, now that I'm no longer employed by the hospital, I no longer have access to the resources to help Bethany get back on her feet."

Saying it out loud to Rourke like that, the full weight of what I've done hits me full in the stomach. Tears prick my eyes as I realize I still haven't told Bethany any of this.

It's not that I regret standing up to Blake. Really I don't. But I'm afraid I am very much going to regret letting Bethany and Paisley down.

"You know," Rourke murmurs, "I wouldn't worry too much about that. Seems to me like Yoda and Bethany are a thing now. Or about to be. Which means Bethany's under the protection of the club. And the club takes care of its own."

"What does that mean?" I ask, swallowing.

"The club's a family. When someone needs help, we come together." He gives me a reassuring nod. "Bethany and Paisley are gonna be okay. You don't need to take that burden on yourself."

I set down the half-eaten burger on my plate, suddenly not feeling very hungry at all.

"I hope so," I mumble. "God, Rourke, I hate to think I just made things worse for them." I shake my head, feeling helpless. "It's bad enough that I just threw away one of the only decent social work jobs in the area. I can't bear to think that I hurt them, too. I'd like to think that something good came out of all of this."

"Plenty of good came out of all this. Mickey's out of the picture. Bethany's free. Paisley's healing up nicely."

"True..." I trail off, still not able to shake the feeling I've let them down.

Rourke cocks his head at me. "What about you? You having second thoughts about quitting?"

I consider his words. "Other than leaving Bethany in the lurch?" I shrug, picking up a fry. "I guess I feel bad I stormed out instead of giving my two weeks, because of the patients I was working with. But besides that? No, not really. Though ask me again in a couple of months when I'm living on canned cat food."

"Better than the kind that comes in a bag," Rourke deadpans.

I almost snort chewed French fry out my nose.

"Nice snort," he says again.

"Whatever. Don't make me snort, and I won't snort."

"So." He leans back in the booth and crosses his arms. "Let's back up. I'm not really clear on what happened when Barber called you into his office. Was he gonna fire you, or something? Is that why you quit?"

I've been trying to avoid giving Rourke the real reason. I guess I'm just embarrassed. I don't want to go down the whole rabbit hole of Blake being jealous, and why. Because that might lead into dangerous territory: Talking about whatever it is that's going on between Rourke and me.

But he's looking at me with an expressions that says he's not going to let me change the subject again.

"Blake saw us this morning," I murmur. "He saw me getting off your bike."

"So?"

"So... I guess after he caught us, um, kissing in the coffee shop that day," I continue, reddening, "he made the assumption we were together, and uh, he didn't like it much."

Rourke locks eyes with me. I can't read his expression at all.

"He didn't, huh? That any of his business?"

"No, obviously not," I say quickly. "But... Blake asked me out a few times when I was first hired. And he's been *persistent* about it." I grimace. "To be honest, it's been sort of exhausting keeping him at arm's length. And I guess his ego was pretty bruised at the thought that I turned him down, but would spend time with you."

So that's why you quit?" Rourke frowns. "Because he was mad you were with me?"

"Well, not exactly..." *Here goes nothing.* "He demanded I completely stop seeing you. Inside the hospital or out. He basically said he wasn't going to have an employee of his hospital consorting with a criminal."

"Consorting?" A corner of his mouth twitches.

"His word."

"So... you quit your job so you could continue 'consorting' with me?" Rourke raises a brow.

"No!" I protest. "I mean, I wouldn't *mind* consorting with you, but..."

Oh, my God, this is possibly the most awkward and embarrassing moment of my life.

"Okay." I blow out a breath and try again. "First of all, can we stop with the word 'consorting'? Second, I quit because I'm not going to be bullied like that. By him or by anybody. It's the principle of the thing. It has nothing to do with whether you and I keep seeing each other or not."

"Nothing?" his eyes twinkle.

"Nothing," I repeat, my jaw jutting.

"Huh."

Rourke leans back in the booth for a moment, lost in thought.

I wait, not sure what he's thinking, and not sure I want to know. God, this is *so* awkward. I almost wish I'd never come here with him today.

"You wanna know something?" he finally says.

"What?"

"I think this is maybe technically our third date."

I snort again, then hold up a hand. "I know, I know! *Don't* say 'nice snort'. But it's kind of funny to call this a date, when it basically started with me being held at gunpoint."

"True." He pauses a second. "You wanna know something else? I've never been on a date before you."

I gape at him. "Really?" I ask, honestly shocked.

"Well," he chuckles, "except for the time I took my sister to her seventh-grade dance, because she told me she was getting bullied. But I don't think that counts."

"If it does, I think you and I have to have a serious talk," I quip.

Rourke bursts into laughter. "That was fucked up, but funny. You're pretty funny, Laney the social worker."

"Ex-social worker," I correct him. "And great. Funny is what every girl strives to be."

He doesn't say anything for a second. When he speaks again, his tone is serious.

"You know how fucking scared I was that I was gonna be too late getting to you today?" he says quietly, leaning forward.

His voice has changed. It's dropped a register. Lower, huskier, more intimate.

It reminds me of the way he talks to me when we're in bed.

I suppress a shiver.

"I was pretty scared, too," I admit. "Thanks, by the way. Did I say thanks already?"

"You done with your food?" he asks, pointing at my abandoned plate. "I think we should get out of here."

I swear I'm starting to get whiplash from all this jumping around from subject to subject. "Yeah, okay," I frown, thoroughly confused.

Rourke throws a couple of bills on the table, and I slide out of the booth. He calls a goodbye to one of the guys behind the bar, and a minute later, I'm sitting on the back of his bike, arms around him as he drives us back in the direction of Ironwood.

I have no idea what's up with Rourke right now, and honestly I'm too afraid to ask. Worried I'll be disappointed in the answer. Belatedly, I kick myself for not making up another story about why I quit my job. A story that didn't involve him. Maybe I freaked him out by basically admitting I wanted to see him again.

The truth is, I feel something for Rourke I've never felt for any man before. And yeah, it's not like I've even had that many relationships. But even so, I know this one is different.

It's important to me.

In fact, it's a lot more important than I've allowed myself to admit, even to myself.

Maybe this is the last time I'll see him. The last time I'll ever be on the back of this bike. I sort of knew it had to end sometime. But it feels so sudden. I'm not ready.

I swallow around a lump in my throat, and look around at the trees and nature whizzing by, trying to take it all in. Trying to fix a mental snapshot of everything, so I can remember it all. How free being on this motorcycle felt. And how free Rourke made me feel. Free, and safe at the same time. And *seen* — for who I actually am. Not Laney, the senator's wayward daughter. Not Laney, the recently unemployed social worker.

Laney, the woman.

The woman who somehow has managed to meet a man who might be everything she's ever wanted, in the last possible place she would have thought.

When we get back into town, I start counting down the minutes until we'll be back at my place, and this will all be over.

But to my surprise, Rourke doesn't turn off the highway when I think he will.

Instead, he keeps going, past downtown, and then even further. We're almost to the turnoff for the clubhouse when he slows and pulls off onto a street I've never been on before. We drive a few blocks more, passing houses that start out tightly packed together, then get more spaced out as we go.

Finally, we come to a dead end, and a long low house set back a bit from the road.

This can only be Rourke's place.

"Laney."

It isn't until he says my name that I realize I'm just sitting on his bike, not moving. I scramble up from the seat, pulling off my helmet as Rourke puts down the kickstand and gets off. I give him a quizzical look, but he's already heading to the front door. He unlocks it and pushes it open, motioning for me to go through.

It isn't until I'm inside that I realize the house abuts a wooded area. The entryway leads immediately to a large, open area that's kitchen, dining room and living room. The back wall is almost entirely floor to ceiling windows, giving the space the feel of a treehouse.

"Wow," I breathe. "This place is amazing."

"Glad you like it."

Rourke stands silently as I wander around the room. I go up to the windows and look outside. It's incredibly peaceful here. In spite of all the trauma and commotion of the day, I feel my muscles untense, a sense of calm coming over me.

When I turn away from the window, Rourke is still standing behind me. He's watching me, dark eyes unreadable. I feel my breath catch in my chest to see him like that — so gorgeous, so masculine. So fully him.

"Rourke," I begin, hardly daring to ask the question. "Why are we here?"

"I wanted to get you away from all the shit," he says simply. "From the club, too. This needs to just be about you and me."

"What does?"

He crosses the room, until he's standing a couple of feet in front of me. He leans against the window glass. The reflection from the outside lightens his eyes, making them almost light gray.

"I've never had a woman here before," he murmurs. "You're the first."

My mouth starts to fall open, but I catch myself. "Ever?"

"Yeah." He takes a step forward. "And you're my first date."

"Except for your sister," I joke.

He smirks. "What I'm trying to say, Laney the ex-social worker, is you're the first for me, in a lot of ways."

He pauses a beat. Then he leans down.

His lips brush mine.

"And dammit, I want more firsts with you," he rumbles.

Then he reaches for me, his eyes shimmering like the only stars in my sky.

And just like that, my heart starts to crash against my ribcage. I've been fighting against believing there could ever be anything more serious between Rourke and me than just a fleeting affair.

I've tried not to indulge a fantasy I knew was crazy. I couldn't imagine what the hell a guy like him would want with someone like me.

Because of that, I've tried hard not to let Rourke think I had any expectations. Not to let *myself* have any.

But now, here he is.

Saying the words I never dared even hope to hear.

"I know we're from different worlds." He puts one arm around me. His other hand comes up to my face, his thumb tracing the line of my jaw more gently than you'd ever expect from such a mountain of a man. "Maybe what I have to offer ain't for you. My world can be dangerous. I know it's not what you're used to. But I promise you one thing, Laney. I will never let the bad parts of that world touch you." His eyes grow dark as coal, fierce and determined. "I'll keep you safe. I guarantee you I will always keep you safe."

As he tilts my face up to his, I think back to the first time I saw Rourke Powers. What I thought about him then.

Huge. Scary. Dangerous. Potentially violent.

How different that is from what I *know* about him now.

Fiercely loyal. Surprisingly kind.

Sexy as hell.

Strong as iron.

A protector.

A man I trust. More than any other man I can think of.

A man I love. Completely, with my whole heart.

"I believe you," I whisper.

Rourke's impossibly dark eyes grow tender, then. They're heartbreakingly beautiful right now. And they're looking right at me. Like I'm the only thing in his universe.

"I've never said these words to any woman, Laney Hart. So here's another first: I'm pretty sure I'm in love you." He shakes his head, and laughs softly. "I'm so fucking in love with you I didn't even see it coming. You hit me like a freight train, babe. You're outspoken, and strong, and you aren't afraid to do what's right. And damned if you don't keep me on my toes."

"Rourke." Despite the warmth of his body, I have goosebumps. "I'm pretty sure I love you, too." As I say the words, for some reason laughter bubbles up from somewhere deep inside me. I'm not sure why.

And then I realize it.

I'm happy.

"Holy fuck," he chuckles again. "This is one hell of a thing, isn't it?"

I laugh and lay my head against his chest, my eyes suddenly wet. "Yes it is," I say softly, breathing in the scent of him. The scent of soap, and leather, and the open road that I already know so well.

It's crazy. All of it is. But looking back, I don't think I'd change one single thing about the way I met Rourke Powers. Not for the world.

Rourke leans down, and kisses me. Deep and slow. My whole center of gravity seems to shift as I return the kiss. I'm dizzy, but grounded. Centered by him.

As he picks me up and carries me to his bedroom, I wrap my arms around his neck, feeling the size, and strength, and heat of him. Everything in the world feels exactly as it's supposed to be. I don't have a job, or a clue what I'm going to do with myself going forward. But I have him. And somehow, I know that's all that really matters.

Whatever our future holds for us together, this is right. I'm sure of that.

More sure than I've ever been of anything

This life with Rourke Powers is going to be a wild ride, I'm sure. One I never could have imagined before we met.

But I know who he is. And I'm pretty sure I know what we have.

It's a first. For both of us. And it's exactly where I want to be. For the rest of my life.

EPILOGUE

ROURKE

"They look like they'll be very happy together," I murmur to Laney as we watch them cut the cake.

"No they won't," she whispers back cheerfully. "But they'll be rich and important, and maybe that means they won't notice it so much."

Laney's sister Lindsay and her new husband Nick stand together beside a wedding cake that's taller than either of them, with so much decoration and frosting that it looks more like a sculpture than anything edible. And I guess that's probably the point. It's got dozens of real-looking flowers cascading down from the top of it, and gold leaf patterns that look more to me like wallpaper than anything, but whatever.

When I said we're watching them "cut" the cake, that's an exaggeration. What we're really watching them do is *pretend* to cut the cake. The two of them stand there, frozen smiles in place, as a group of photographers wind all around them, taking pictures of their rings, their hands on the knife, looking into each other's eyes, her pretending to laugh at a joke he's pretending to tell... Jesus Christ, it goes on forever. We all stand around pretending to give a shit, while we're just waiting for the whole goddamn thing to be over.

Or maybe that's just me.

Thank God I managed to make friends with one of the bartenders earlier. He's got a bottle of Jack back behind the bar with my name on it. That bottle may be the only way I manage to get through this reception, I swear to Christ.

Laney told me they even have a social media consultant for this thing. Hashtag wedding of the fucking century, or some shit like that.

Laney's sister and her new husband finally cut the goddamn cake. We all raise our drinks and clap for them while the photographers take pictures. I notice none of them are aiming their cameras at Laney and me. My bet is, they've been told to keep us out of the photos as much as possible. Suits me just fine.

Laney's family, man... they're really something else. Her mom is so uptight, it actually looks like someone's surgically implanted a broomstick up her ass. She doesn't give a single opinion on anything in Laney's dad's presence without looking at him for approval.

Her dad, Senator Hart, smells like money — the dirty kind. He's a silver-haired southern politician right out of central casting, shaking hands, kissing babies, and laughing this big, fake-ass booming laugh. But even his flawless southern hospitality doesn't quite extend to the likes of me. When Laney introduced me to him and her mom last night at the rehearsal dinner, I swear I thought they were gonna call the whole wedding off just so they wouldn't have to deal with the scandal of having their older daughter show up on my fuckin' arm.

And I even broke down and wore a suit for this.

The whole family, Laney's sister included, was pretty much horrified to see her arrive with the likes of me. I'm pretty sure they already thought Laney was as much of a disappointment to them as she could be, but I guess we've done a damn good job of proving them wrong. I am clearly their worst fucking nightmare. It's pretty obvious it's killing them to have all their rich society friends see Laney show up on the arm of a guy with tattoos and grease under his nails.

It's hilarious how fuckin' scandalized these assholes all are. But the best part is, Laney's at least as amused by it as I am.

And even though if there's a hell, it will probably be an eternity of this fucking wedding, I wouldn't miss being here with Laney. I love watching her give zero fucks when her mom gives her the side-eye for not playing the good little senator's daughter. It cracked me up to see her parents flip their shit when she left her chair at the head table during dinner to come sit with me in the cheap seats.

Looking at her now, with her hair all pulled up away from her face, smiling up at me, Laney's the most beautiful woman in the whole damn room. She even puts the bride to shame. Whatever her family thinks of her, everyone here can see it.

And she's all mine.

STANDING NEXT to her now among all the other guests, a glass of champagne in her hand and a beer in mine, I can't help but laugh at how different this weekend is from last weekend.

The Lords had a fundraiser for Paisley and Bethany, to help them pay for Paisley's hospital stay. The entire club was there, helping out. Hell, even Laney's friend Katie the nurse was there. I'm pretty sure she still doesn't like me all that much, but I think she might be starting to come around. We didn't manage to raise enough to wipe the whole hospital bill out, but we came damn close. And from what Yoda says, he and Bethany will be able to pay off the rest by the end of the year.

Bethany moved in with Yoda a couple months after I convinced Laney to move into my place. Bethany fits right in with the club, and Yoda's one happy motherfucker. Paisley's arm healed up just fine, and she's doing great. She and Addi are pretty much best friends, too. Which is great for Paisley, because now she's a cool kid by association at Ironwood Elementary. She doesn't get bullied anymore.

As for Mickey, well... he's long gone. Skipped town, just like that. At least, that's what Yoda told Bethany. And for all intents and purposes, that's what I told Laney, too.

The truth? Well, that's a little more gruesome. But hell, he's alive. He should consider himself damn lucky for that, the piece of shit. And since he jumped bail, he's wanted for arrest in Ohio. Not to mention, he's wanted by Jimmy Mazur, too, for failure to repay his loan.

I guess the Vietnamese got to him after we did. Turns out, Jimmy's not the only one he still owed money to. They got their payback, though, from what I hear. With interest.

Let's just say Mickey will never flip anyone the bird again.

I think it's pretty safe to say, we ain't likely to see Mickey King around here anymore.

Speaking of Mazur, it didn't take much convincing from the club to get him to decide to leave Bethany alone. He let her quit dancing at his club without giving her any trouble, too — with a little strong-arming from Yoda and me, that is.

Laney and Bailey helped Bethany put together a résumé, and got her some decent interview clothes. With Bailey as a reference, she ended up getting a job in the main office of Ironwood Elementary School. So not only does Bethany now work during the hours Paisley's at school, she doesn't even have to pay for daycare. Win-win.

As for Laney, it turned out that when word got around she had quit at the hospital — and why — the women on staff started talking. Long story short, a bunch of them brought sexual harassment charges against Blake Barber. They called Laney about it, and she added her name to the suit. At first Barber vowed to fight it, but I guess his lawyer ended up talking him out of it. Eventually he agreed to resign if the women would drop the whole thing.

Once Barber left, the interim director was more than happy to re-hire Laney to her old position. She's thrilled to be back.

And me? I'm happy as hell for her.

JUST LIKE WITH THE CAKE, it takes forever for the photographers to stage the bouquet toss. As they assemble all the unmarried women in a group, I stand off to one side, nursing my beer and watching the hoity-toity shitshow in front of me with amusement. I wonder whether they're gonna do this shit a bunch of times too, so they can get it from every angle. But in the end, I guess that's too fuckin' ridiculous, even for them.

With a big, wide smile, Lindsay turns her back away from the crowd of women, winds up, and tosses the bouquet behind her.

In exactly the opposite direction from Laney.

Some chick on the other side of the group catches the thing, and everyone starts clapping and screaming like she just won the goddamn lottery. Beaming, Lindsay goes over to take a shitload of pictures with the lucky winner.

Laney turns and rolls her eyes at me. I wink.

"God, could that have been any more obvious?" she laughs when she's back by my side. "I bet all the women who stood by me are just kicking themselves. They should have known better."

"You think they all wanna get married that bad?"

"No," she laughs. "But did you see how many pictures Lindsay took with the one who caught it? That's prime social media real estate, being in a picture with the bride of the season!"

"LOL," I quip.

"By the way, you are really rocking that suit," Laney tells me with a grin. "And I'm not the only one who thinks so. Do you know, every one of Lindsay's bridesmaids has been stealing glances at you, trying not to openly lust? I think they can't decide whether to admire me or hate me for being with you."

"Well, don't get used to it. This monkey suit is coming off as soon as I can manage it."

"Ooh. Is that a promise?" she says, elbowing me and wiggling her eyebrows.

"It is." I turn and give her a look. "You wanna ditch this reception and go back to the hotel?"

"Do I?" she practically squeals. "Take me away from all of this, and I'll be forever in your debt."

We slip out of the party a few minutes later. I open the passenger door of Laney's car and help her inside, then go around and get into the driver's seat. She heaves a sigh of contentment and pulls off her shoes, murmuring how happy she is to be out of there.

As I'm driving back to the hotel, I find myself thinking about a wedding of our own. Oh, not like this one. I know without even asking Laney that this isn't her scene. Besides, her family will probably be so fucking scandalized if and when we decide to get married, they'll probably all have a collective heart attack and refuse to come.

My sister Regan will be on board though. I know that for a fact. Laney and I rode out to visit her at college about a month ago, and the two of them got along like a house on fire. Regan would love to have Laney as a sister-in-law. Especially since we basically don't have any other family.

The drive to the hotel is short, and we make it in comfortable silence, each of us lost in our thoughts. When we get there, we go up to our room, and I do to her what I've been dying to do ever since I saw her in that red dress.

"Be careful with the zipper," she says breathlessly, turning her head to look over her shoulder as I struggle with it. "I rented this dress through one of those online companies. It has to go back soon, and I'll get charged if it's damaged."

I'm actually disappointed. "You mean I'm not gonna see this thing on you again?"

"I mean..." she looks at me coyly through lowered lashes as I unzip the thing down to her waist, then turns around. "We still have a couple more days with it..."

A low chuckle rumbles up through my throat as I slide my hands over the smooth, silky fabric covering her curves. It's soft, but it's got nothing on her skin. "In that case, I'm not gonna vouch for this thing making it back unscathed."

I slip one hand under the skirt, gripping her thigh and pulling her back into me, so my cock is pressing against her ass. She moans and leans into me, and I reach around, sliding a finger under the lacy black thong I know she's got under there. She stiffens, letting out a little gasp, as I find her wet and ready.

"Fuck me, Laney. I'll never get tired of this," I growl, my own voice tight as I struggle to contain myself. "I'll never get tired of you. Of us."

She turns her head back to me, and I kiss her from behind as I swirl my fingers around her swollen, needy pussy. Her hips thrust toward my hand, riding the rhythm, her body trusting me. I don't know how the fuck it happens, but every single time we do this, it just gets better and better. I love hearing the way she moans my name. I love making her gasp, making her body respond under my touch. I love everything about this.

I fucking love everything about *her*.

Somehow I manage to get her out of that dress, and then we're a tangle of bodies, skin to skin. I make her come, bucking against my tongue, tasting her sweet juices. Then I pull her against me, entering her up to the hilt. For a second, I have to close my eyes against the pleasure so I don't fucking lose it. Then we find the dance that's all ours — her hips flexing against me as I move inside her, heat gathering, ready to combust. She locks eyes with me, her lips parting as her breathing gets shallower, more ragged. The pressure builds inside me, unstoppable. Then, suddenly, her nails dig into my thighs, her lids fluttering shut as she tightens and comes again, moaning my name as she pulses around me. I release inside her, white hot pleasure washing over me like a tidal wave.

Just like she does every night, Laney falls asleep in my arms. I listen to her deep, even breathing, and lie there, thinking about what a lucky fucking bastard I am.

Call me a romantic. Call me whatever the fuck you want. But I'm gonna make this woman my wife.

Because no matter what our future holds — what we have is real. It's solid.

And it's rare as shit.

Yep. I'm one of the lucky ones.

And I want her to know I know it. Every time she looks in my eyes. And every time she looks down at the ring I'm gonna put on her finger one day soon.

I love her, and always will. Now, and forever.

DAPHNE TALKS OUT HER ASS ABOUT IRON WILL

So, recently, I've started doing this thing where at the end of my books, I'll just ramble on for a little bit about something that was happening while I was writing the book in question. Sometimes it will give you a little insight on how I developed a character, or something that happens during a scene, or a song that inspired me. And sometimes it's just me talking out my ass.

Hence, the title of this section.

The thing that happened while I was writing this book was that I actually started using Instagram.

I mean, I had an account, because someone told me I had to. So I signed up, and looked around, and I was like, *What the hell is this thing even for?*

I mean, don't mock me. I know I'm a late adopter. What can I say? I'm a recluse weirdo writer. I consider my cats my co-workers.

But I had started to spend a little more time on the platform around Christmas. And then, I happened to hear about this TV show streaming on Netflix called *You*. Well, I found out that *You* was based on a book, and I'm the type of person who always likes to read the book first if I possibly can. So I grabbed a copy of *You* off Amazon and devoured it in a single day. (If you haven't read or seen this thing, it's creepy, y'all. But really good, too.)

The female main character in the book is called Guinevere Beck — but everyone just calls her Beck. In the book, especially, she's on Twitter and Instagram kind of all the time — she wants to be an "influencer." And so I was reading this book at the same time that I was exploring Instagram more as a platform and finally starting to learn what it was about. Sometimes, weird little coincidences happen like that in an author's life, and often, they end up making it into a book in some way.

So, that's how, when I "discovered" while writing this book that Laney has a little sister, I also discovered that she's a young socialite and a social media influencer. And that is how, for the first time ever in a book, I actually use a hashtag.

#authorlearningnewthings

Oh, and one more thing: Follow me on Instagram! LOL
https://www.instagram.com/daphneloveling/

ABOUT DAPHNE LOVELING

Daphne Loveling is a small-town girl who moved to the big city as a young adult in search of adventure. She lives in the American Midwest with her fabulous husband and the two cats who own them.

Someday, she hopes to retire to a sandy beach and continue writing with sand between her toes.

CPSIA information can be obtained
at www.ICGtesting.com
Printed in the USA
LVHW110502260319
611853LV00001B/131/P

9 781090 224156